Home
Away
from Home

Home
Away
from Home

Lorna J. Cook

St. Martin's Press ⚇ New York

HOME AWAY FROM HOME. Copyright © 2005 by Lorna J. Cook. All rights reserved. Printed in the United States of America. No part of this book may be used or reproduced in any manner whatsoever without written permission except in the case of brief quotations embodied in critical articles or reviews. For information, address St. Martin's Press, 175 Fifth Avenue, New York, N.Y. 10010.

www.stmartins.com

Book design by Irene Vallye

"Separation" copyright © by W. S. Merwin, reprinted with the permission of the Wylie Agency Inc.

ISBN 0-312-30819-1
EAN 978-0312-30819-3

First Edition: January 2005

10 9 8 7 6 5 4 3 2 1

For my parents

Acknowledgments

I am very grateful to the following people: Lisa Bankoff, my agent, and Dori Weintraub, my editor, for their care and vision; Tina DuBois, ICM assistant, and Yolanda Vega, at the Hope College Upward Bound, for helpful insights. Also, for necessary and often extraordinary support, I am indebted to the Nyenhuis and Cook families; Wendy Willoughby; Michele Lonergan; Carla Vissers; friends near and far-flung; and most of all, to Chris and Simon and Justis, who are my home.

SEPARATION

Your absence has gone through me
Like thread through a needle.
Everything I do is stitched with its color.

—W. S. MERWIN, *The Moving Target*

Home
Away
from Home

I used to make lists every day. A satisfying scribble, neat columns of tasks—to do, to buy, to fix—and, sometimes, an inventory of my strengths and weaknesses. One of the latter was a propensity for cheating on my lists; I would scratch out "Monday" and write "Tuesday" at the top, mentally letting myself off the hook. However, if I wrote something down, eventually I would check it off the list. My husband, Dill, called it the Triage Report, mocking the way I took so seriously the need to tend to things, to prioritize. Then I discovered that, no matter how organized you are or how carefully you think you are living your life, things have a way of getting out of your control. The lid slips off and everything you saved and loved and counted on whirls away in the wind.

It was late November, and I'd had on my fix-it list for several days running "Call garage door repair," because our car had been held hostage in the garage by a faulty spring in the automatic-door pulley. Such a small, inconsequential thing, a tiny cog, yet it dramatically impeded my orderly lifestyle. Even so, I neglected to phone for a repair immediately (not at the top of my list) and simply rode my bike to work. The weather was unseasonably mild for a Michigan autumn, and riding was a nice change. Dill, a graphic designer, had an office at home, so he didn't care; when I told him I'd forgotten to get the door fixed, he tilted back in his purple desk chair and shrugged.

"Maybe we should simplify," he said.

"Simplify?" I laughed. "This from a man who already wears the same shirt three days straight."

"I don't get that dirty," he said, frowning down at his soft blue oxford. I admit, I loved that shirt. It smelled of soap and sleep and fresh air. Dill reached for my hand and pulled me closer so my hip rested on the back of his chair. It was one of those old courthouse chairs with a swivel, stripped and painted a garish plum color that had chipped and faded so that it had a pleasing lived-in appearance, a kind of functional sculpture of which my husband's body was often a part. He wrapped an arm around my waist. "I was just thinking," he said dreamily. "We could sell the car, the house, quit our jobs. Run away together."

"Where?" I asked, humoring him.

"I don't know—Muskegon?"

I laughed. Muskegon was thirty miles north of McKinley along Lake Michigan, where we lived, and an even smaller, more odorous town. McKinley, which manufactures peppermints, held a superior attitude toward its neighbor, with its rancid paper pulp. When the neighboring high-school teams competed, the McKinleyites liked to shout, "You stink!" even if they themselves lost by a landslide, which they often did, in basketball, football, and even swimming. Dill was once a member of the McKinley High School swim team, and he joked that none of them knew how to swim because they spent their summers wading into the freezing lake, never going further than knee-deep.

"So, what do you say, gorgeous—want to take a chance on me?" Dill said.

"Sure, why not," I said, kissing the top of his head. "Let me know when to start packing."

Later, much later, I remembered that moment and wished I had stayed at his side. I wished I had noticed how perfect he was; you should never take for granted the softness of a shirt, the squeakiness of an old chair, the scent of Magic Markers and soap, and the gentle gaze of the one you love. You should notice the one you love.

After dinner we got busy with our own work—his deadline, my student list for the new semester. He went to bed before I did, complaining of a headache, and in the morning I left before he was awake.

By the time I got home from work that day, Dill was slumped over in front of the television, which was tuned to a Spanish-speaking channel. Sorrowful music was swelling on the *telenovela*, and a woman was weeping and banging on a man's chest. He was holding her at bay, imploring her to who-knows-what, since regrettably, I don't speak Spanish; now it seems important, like a message I never received.

There was an open bottle of aspirin spilled on the carpet like little teeth. I grabbed Dill and yelled his name; he moaned. Then I reached for the phone to call for help but Dill came around before I dialed.

"Hey," he said, so softly it sounded like he was in another room.

"What happened? What's wrong?" I was kneeling beside him, holding too tightly to his arm (wanting to pinch him), searching his face for signs, symptoms, though I didn't know what I was looking for.

"I don't know. I had a headache again when I woke up and took some—" He struggled to speak, waved a hand as if playing charades.

"Aspirin?" I said.

He nodded, then leaned over and held his head in his hands. "I think I need a doctor," he said.

"Let's go," I said, pulling him to his feet. He followed obediently, leaning on me heavily. At the back door, he slipped on a throw rug and his legs scissored. I caught him, dragging the rug with us to the threshold. Once we were outside, I pushed open the side door to the garage and got Dill to the car. "It's okay, you're going to be okay," I said firmly, yanking open the door while supporting him. Tall and lean, Dill had never struck me as heavy before.

"I have a headache," he said again, but his eyes were drooping, then rolling in their sockets. As soon as I got him into the car, he collapsed. And then I realized what I had done. I pounded on the automatic door opener on the dashboard, but it only buzzed and the garage door stayed shut tight as a coffin. By then I was too exhausted to try to pull him back out, so I left him there and ran into the house to dial 911.

While I waited for an ambulance, I went back to sit with my comatose husband. I kept patting his cheek, trying to keep wake him. I said, "Dammit, how could you? How could you be so stupid?" and other cruel things over and over till the police and rescue sirens came screaming into the driveway. Of course, I was talking to myself. How could I have done something so wrong, so devastatingly wrong?

For seventeen hours, Dill slumbered peacefully in intensive care. I sat nearby and watched him until my eyes burned. His skin grew faintly oily and his hair plastered to his forehead, so I found a towel and wiped it with cool water. "Hey," I whispered. "Hey, you." I said it softly, lovingly, as if sending myself through each small syllable. He slept on.

The attending physician, Dr. Milner, had called in a neurologist named Dr. Baird, who swept into the hospital with coattails flapping and a hand running across his blond buzz-cut hair. He rallied a small army of nurses and radiologists, who scattered with their instructions as if on a scavenger hunt. He spoke softly to me, hinting at impossible things like brain tumors and meningitis, or viruses that had no name. It alarmed me that an expert could be so vague and uncertain. "It could be any one of a number of things. We have to rule out the worst, first," he said. What was the worst? I wondered but dared not ask.

I knew my mother was waiting in the mauve-carpeted lobby along with a couple of my friends, and finally I went to find them and tell them to go home, that I would stay, and Dill would be fine. On the way down the hallway I stopped in the rest room to splash cold water on my face, pressing a paper towel to my eyelids. I took time to pee, and even to check my face in the mirror afterward. When Dill woke, I thought, this was what he would see. A sight for sore eyes, he would say, blatantly lying. I dug around in my purse for some lipstick and rubbed a little of it on my cheeks. Then I washed my hands, opened the door, and was intercepted by Dr. Baird.

"—brain aneurysm," he was saying. "It erupted quite suddenly, unexpectedly. Like a firecracker."

I waited, baffled. I felt like someone in need of a translator; the words were slow to reach my mind; I did not know what he was telling me or why.

"There were no previous symptoms, it seems. It happens this way sometimes," he said, though his expression indicated that, until now, he had never seen it happen this way. "You didn't notice anything unusual in the past few weeks?" He seemed strangely nervous, anxious, as if his mask of calm had slipped off. I shook my head. I hadn't noticed anything. Everything was just the way it had always been and always would be. As soon as Dill came home. But what the doctor was telling me, in his awkward yet thorough way, was that Dill was not coming home. He had, in fact, just left without saying good-bye, in the few moments I was away from his side, while I washed my face in the restroom, while I put on lipstick.

"I'm very, very sorry" were the doctor's words, each hitting at close range, exploding inside me. Everything went black and I woke in a white hospital room myself, alone, with flowers bobbing toward me from a vase.

It was raining. It always rains at burials, it seems, as if the clusters of mourners in their dark clothes and drawn faces pull the clouds down around them.

I stood bolstered by friends like bookends, though I was not really there, of course. I was floating just off to the side, near a tombstone carved with twin angels, watching the dream unfold. I wanted to be able to remember it later when I woke: *Dill, this is so weird, but you were in a casket, so polished it glowed. It was eerie. And it was raining, just a gray mist like wet fog. There were a lot of people I never expected to see, like your college roommate, Danny, can you believe it? Who called him, I wonder. And your mother couldn't stand up; someone brought a folding chair for her. I was thinking how she hates flying and that she even once said, "Only for your funeral," when you tried to get her to visit. I was standing with Lexi and Jillian and some other people, and I wondered if your mother remembered saying that. The minister was the one from the Presbyterian church on Fourth Street. He was crying, it was really touching, and it made me cry in my dream, as if it were real.*

But, of course, it wasn't.

The day after the funeral I moved back home with my mother. I had wanted just to lie down, and I happened to be at my mother's house when the feeling hit me. So I lay down in my old room—half preserved like a shrine with my stuffed animals gray with age and my bulletin board still covered with photos torn from *Seventeen* magazines, the other half stacked with boxes destined for Goodwill. I stared at everything through a fog of dismay and disbelief, a dense layer of grief. Falling backward in my life, I stared for hours at my walls covered with teenage models. Their glossed lips remained forever shiny. Their eyes gleamed with happiness as they posed in their back-to-school plaids and blonde whiplash braids. Now what? I thought, and closed my watering eyes.

"We got a new mattress," my mother said when she walked into my room and looked at me. Apparently, it was all she could think to say by way of comfort. I noticed that she was still speaking of herself as part of a pair, though my father had been dead for nine years. I wondered if I would start doing that. Perhaps my mother's way of dealing with my father's absence was to pretend he was just away—for a long, long time.

When I was young, I used to watch my parents sitting together at the kitchen table late at night, or nestled on the sofa watching Johnny Carson. I was quiet and stealthy; they never noticed me then, so wrapped up in their companionable conversations, or even silences. I marveled at how two such different people—my father a textbook editor, cerebral and well-read, my mother a seamstress who favored television and magazines—could be so inseparable. As their only child, I was drawn into their little circle, but as a kind of appendage, an offshoot, not really part of the whole. On road trips I sat in the backseat by myself, listening to their lulling talk, wondering how they could find so much to say. Sometimes my mother would turn around to ask how I was doing, hand me a coloring book or a snack, and my father would angle the rearview mirror to get a look at me, as if he had forgotten I was there. He was kind and soft-spoken, a little aloof, my mother cheerful though sometimes offhandedly careless. My father read to me at night and glanced at my homework, and my mother took care of me the way mothers do; I was always clean and fed and dressed, always had a Halloween costume (her specialty), and birthday cakes and school supplies. But though we spent the most time together, since my father was at work or conferences, my mother didn't seem to really know me. She asked about school and feigned interest in my small world, but I sensed as I grew that my mother didn't want to be bothered by any real problems I might have. How I learned about sex and racism and even religion is a mystery to me. My parents both seemed to assume that I was turning out fine, like a plant that needed occasional watering. And I suppose, in my placidness, I gave them reason not to worry or pay too much attention.

When my father died so suddenly, the circle that was our family changed, pushing together my mother and me in a way we never had been. After his funeral, I found myself tending to her, picking up her clothes from the floor, reminding her to eat. I was twenty-five, self-sufficient and independent. My mother's new neediness alarmed me. I didn't want to be there, trying futilely to fill in the gap left by my father, her other half. And she seemed cut in half, diminished, and there was nothing I could do but flit around the edges of her grief and attempt to keep her afloat until the worst of it passed.

Now here we were, our roles shifting once again. My mother sat down and began raking her nails through my uncombed hair. She said, "Anna, if you need to talk, I'm here." And then she left.

I couldn't form any words yet; they were frozen inside me under layers and layers of snow. Every morning I'd shovel a path to get through the day, but by evening, it would be covered over again.

Friends called and dropped by regularly, but I refused to see any of them. They left a pile of note cards and flowers and carefully packaged baked goods. I could hear the phone ringing, the door opening and latching again. I could hear the low, sorrowful murmur of their voices, though not their words. I didn't want to hear them. I wanted to pretend I was a child home sick from school—but my imagination never was that strong. So I simply closed my eyes again and tried not to think at all. I had arranged a leave of absence from work; vaguely I'd promised my boss I would return in a few weeks, maybe a month. She was more than sympathetic; she said, "Take all the time you need." If I'd taken her literally, I might have stayed in bed for the rest of my life.

It was a long, tedious dream. Time has a way of changing form, slippery and metamorphic, a slow-motion clock ticking loudly, interminably in your head, and then suddenly zipping away, a train pulling away the hours, days, and weeks before you even notice. My hair grew, my nails grew, jagged and unkempt, and though sometimes I remembered to take a shower and change my clothes, I mostly stayed anchored to my bed waiting for the impossible—for Dill to show up and take me back home.

The holidays came and went while I slept and woke and wept and slept some more on the new mattress, and my mother offered me crackers and cheese and glasses of eggnog. She had enough sense not to overdo it the way she usually did, with tinsel and glitter. I suspected she was eager to string up one more strand of colored lights to try to cheer me up, but she consoled herself with rearranging her collection of Snowbabies on the coffee table and listening to Mel Tormé. On New Year's Eve she made a feeble toast: "To better times," then drank her champagne with gusto, as if I weren't even there. Then she came over and hugged me and wept into my neck.

I pulled away and said, "I'm okay, Mom, really," and went to drink more champagne in my room after she was asleep, quickly, so that it made me feel nauseated and woozy. Eventually I collapsed as if hit over the head. I understood why depressed people sometimes drank; it hastened the escape from consciousness.

I woke in the middle of the night and said hoarsely, "Dill?" There was no answer, so I slid my hand over to the other side of the bed, expecting to find him there while at the same moment the horror of realization thundered through me. I gasped. I curled into a fetal ball under the blankets and hugged myself so hard I had small bruises on my shins the next morning. I thought of Dill's body warm beside me, the weight of his flank pressed against my side, the width of his back I knew by heart, the freckles here, the soft hairs there, the scattering of pale birthmarks that looked like spilled chocolate milk across his lower belly. I knew his scent, the soft sound of his sleeping breath, the shape of each tooth when he smiled, the gray-green of his eyes, the lashes darker than you'd expect against his fair skin. I had gazed on his form awake and asleep for so many days nights mornings, that I knew him better than myself in some ways. I never scrutinized my body the way I memorized his, because I loved him so.

About a week before he died, when everything was so blindingly normal, Dill was getting undressed for bed. "Look at this," he said, tugging at a little fold of flesh at his waist. He was sitting on the bed, in just underwear and socks.

"I can't look at that, I'm too distracted by *that*," I said, pointing to his black socks on his pale legs.

He grinned. "Do you like it? I was thinking it would be my new look. Maybe with sandals?"

I shoved him back onto the bed then and climbed on top of him. "How about when you're eighty?" I suggested.

"Oh, you won't be around when I'm eighty," he said. "You'll have moved on to some younger guy by then."

"No, I won't," I protested, as if he were being serious. "I told you, for better or for worse." I leaned down and kissed him.

"So, even when I'm wearing black socks with shorts *and* I'm fat?"

"Even then." I rolled off him and went to brush my teeth. When I returned, he was still lying there, refusing to remove the socks, smiling beatifically.

As I lay in the dark at my mother's house I whispered, "Come back, come back, come back," a desperate appeal, which comforted as much as pained me somehow, as if by my saying it enough, he might hear me.

When I stumbled downstairs for breakfast around noon the next day, my mother took one look at me, opened her mouth, and then closed it again. She poured me a cup of coffee with a trembling hand and I drank it, tasting nothing, feeling nothing. The numbness was all I could hope for, and I accepted it as a gift.

When the Christmas tree was laid beside the curb, a week after the new year, I decided it was time I stood up and moved on. Some friends had arranged to get my garage door unstuck and my car released. It had sat in my mother's driveway, untouched now for seven weeks. When I got in, the engine protested for just a moment, then rattled and began to hum. I watched the windshield wipers brush off crusty snow while my mother gazed at me forlornly, her hand on the open car window. I touched her sleeve, clung for just a second to its hem like a small child.

"Take care of yourself, sweetheart," she said, and I let go.

"Don't worry about me. I just have to get my feet back on the ground."

I knew I could not go back to our home, our rugs, his shoes, his toothbrush dangling in the bathroom. I couldn't walk through the rooms Dill had walked through, sit in chairs he had sat in, and definitely not sleep in the bed where he had slept beside me for six years. I had to find another place to be, to live. And it turned out there wasn't any one such place, so by trial and error, I made my way.

When you live in a small town, as I do, it takes effort to redraw your paths, to start over. However, if you are also grieving, people tend to give you a wide berth; they expect you to behave erratically so that the way you deal with your sorrow becomes your own particular mark. Some are stoic, going back to their routines as quickly as possible—especially if they have children, for the sake of the children—and others withdraw. My way of coping was to become intentionally homeless, though I always had a place to stay. Everyone I asked took me in, so like Blanche DuBois, I learned to rely on the kindness of strangers. Actually, friends; I was the stranger. Without Dill as my mate, my friend, my reflection, I no longer knew who I was. I felt I was falling down a hole, passing through a mirror, never knowing where I might end up or how long I would stay.

When the time came to move on, I just knew and I went.

My friend Lexi, who was divorced with a four-year-old daughter named Penny, was the kind of friend who welcomed strays, her pet axiom being *Mi casa es su casa.* When I stood peering through the window of the back door, she yanked it open and smiled, without a trace of the dismay or pity I had grown used to from some other friends. She engulfed me in her wonderful cinnamony scent and large, soft breasts.

"It's only for a few days," I said when she took my luggage from my hands.

Of course, she cut me off. "Nonsense. You are staying as long as you want to. I could use the company anyway. Penny's not a stellar conversationalist. I need someone who can really talk over a glass of wine, you know?" We had tea, because it was only early afternoon, and Penny was hanging around. Lexi didn't like to drink around her child; she explained, "I don't want her to grow up and remember me sitting at the table brooding. I brood when I drink."

"I brood all the time," I said. I was not normally so flippant; it was a side of me I wasn't sure I liked, but I had no control over it. Lexi patted my arm, then left her hand there for a long moment, so I could feel the pressure of her fingers, her warmth. I thought, That's what love is, the physical imprint of one person on another—a touch, a scent, a voice. I tried not to think about the absence of it in my life, and how much I wanted Lexi to leave her hand there on my arm, maybe all night. Fortunately, Penny broke the mood. She galloped into the kitchen on an inverted mop, hanging on to the dirty strands of rope and yelling, "Whoa, Nellie!" She came to a halt beside my chair and looked me over. "Hello," she said politely.

"Hello, Penny."

"Penny, this is Anna, remember?" her mother said. I felt bad then, knowing I hadn't been around much in the past year, busy with work, my life, such as it was, before. Lexi and I had known each other since high school and remained close, though we drifted in and out of contact over the years. Our husbands didn't get along—Dill was the first to suspect Tom's infidelity and he hated being around him—so we didn't socialize as couples. After the divorce, I met Lexi for lunch regularly, letting her spew her rage; when she seemed settled in her single parenthood, preoccupied with her daughter's care, we drifted apart again. In the meantime, Penny had evolved from a chubby toddler to a sprightly preschooler, a startling transformation, as if Lexi had traded in one child for another.

"You've grown," I said to Penny.

"I know it," she said. "I got a pony."

"Does it have a name?"

"Pony-girl," Penny said, stroking the mop lovingly.

Lexi smiled at her daughter, then pulled her toward a chair. "Why don't you have some tea, okay? Anna and I need to talk."

Penny sat down, hoisting herself up on her knees. She leaned over to try to help herself to the teapot, but Lexi intervened. The teapot was chipped and shaped like a pig, and Penny began oinking while her mother poured, then laughing uproariously at herself. Lexi ignored her and turned to me. "You know, it wasn't your fault. We always think it is, somehow. But it isn't."

Penny repeated "But it isn't" over and over in a little singsong till her mother gently whacked her arm.

"I mean it, Anna," Lexi said.

"I know," I said, but I didn't really know. And much as I loved my friend for her candor and support, I resented her for pricking the sore spot without warning. I wasn't prepared to dissect Dill's death or my feelings about it. He lay deep within Restlawn Cemetery while I sat at a wooden table watching a small girl pet a mop and stack sugar cubes into little villages. It couldn't be true—life couldn't be this strange, this awful—and I wanted to just sit and watch the steam swirling from my cup and say nothing, time circling in a tiny holding pattern overhead.

Eventually, Penny got bored and danced out of the room. I could hear her sifting through a mound of plastic toys, searching for something. Lexi turned back to me, intent. "There wasn't anything you could have done," she said.

"Yes, there was," I snapped. But I couldn't let myself start to list what I could have done. *If only,* I had said ten thousand times. Lexi stayed silent, and I assumed she was searching her brain for the correct response, but of course, there was none. There were no guidebooks for this, I was certain. I stood up and said simply, "I'm really tired."

Lexi led me to her guest room, which doubled as a study—Lexi was the eternal student, forever working on a dissertation while running a catering business, planning to toss it all when she became a Ph.D. in history. Beside the paper-mounded desk, there was a twin bed with a thick comforter faded to the color of melted orange sherbet. Lexi left me with a pile of novels and some outdated political magazines, and went to run a hot bath.

"Why is she in there so long? When can *I* take a bath?" came Penny's muffled whining through the bathroom door. I had soaked until the water was tepid and my fingertips resembled an alien's. I stood up, dripping, and caught a glimpse of myself in the mirror. It was shocking. I hadn't realized I'd lost so much weight, or that dark shadows had begun to ring my eyes.

After Penny was happily bathed and tucked into bed, Lexi poured me a glass of wine. I thought of all the liquids I had consumed in the weeks since my husband's death. People seemed to find comfort in beverages. *Here, have some tea. How about a nice cup of coffee? Let's open some wine. Do you need anything? Water?*

"I have a fatty pot roast in the oven right now, with potatoes," Lexi was saying. "We'll get you back into fighting shape in no time."

I didn't tell her that there was no use fighting. It's easier just to take it. Swallow your pride and all your hopes. Turn the other cheek. Surrender, Dorothy. I took a long sip of wine, and then I surrendered. Lexi scooted over on the sofa to hold me in her arms and murmur "There, there" in just the right tone as I wept.

I ate the pot roast, and all of the potatoes, and the next day I ate two bowls of sticky oatmeal. After five days of bingeing and weeping, and then trying to act cheerful in front of Penny, I had had enough. Lexi, ever gracious, begged me to stay, but I think she must have been relieved to see me go. Penny watched from the front window, cheerily waving Pony-girl at me as I drove away.

For two weeks I alighted at the home of Amy and Ted, old friends with two black Labrador retrievers that lay over our feet like mufflers while we talked.

Amy said, awkwardly, "Is there anything we can do?"

Ted cleared his throat and looked away as if a sign might appear on the wall.

I said nothing. Sometimes I nodded or shook my head. It was as if I'd taken a vow of silence, and I enjoyed it in a strange way. Neither of them seemed to think it odd and they discreetly left me alone. They gave me towels and hot tea, and I borrowed slippers and robes, turned my cheek to an unfamiliar pillowcase, and woke up feeling displaced and guilty, a little like Goldilocks. I wandered through the home of my friends with my back against the walls, trying not to consume too much space.

When I was a child I liked to hide in the cherry tree at the end of my driveway, climbing high enough to go unnoticed yet still view everyone who passed below. The notion of being invisible thrilled me.

I liked to imagine I was a superhero, capable of performing impossible acts. Experimentally, I would extend my arms as I stood on a wide limb, never worrying that I might fall. I half-believed I really could do it, fly right out of the tree, if I wanted to. Sometimes, feeling bold in my hidden perch, I would shoot shriveled fruit at passersby, who would whip around, searching in vain for the culprit. Mostly, though, I just watched them.

Observing rituals that were nothing like my own, in other people's homes, was like that, hiding in plain sight, feeling invisible. The days blurred together—the days, the faces, and the rooms—and I tried to focus on the details, like the preparation of tea. I remembered how Lexi filled the kettle to sputtering every time, and I'd discovered that she had an entire china tea set, like a child's, in addition to the pig. She filled the bowl with sugar cubes and retrieved them with silver tongs, though Penny would resume her building with sticky hands and afterward Lexi would scoop the nicked cubes back into the bowl. At Amy and Ted's there was a basket of herbal tea bags, which we dipped into lukewarm water. It took a long time for the water to develop a tint. We sipped while making small talk about local news. Amy spoke a little too brightly about the proposed library expansion while my mind wandered over all of Dill's books left on our shelves, his fingerprints invisibly covering them. I thought, How can he just be *gone*? I wanted to ask this out loud but thought better of it, knowing how the words would hang in the air, forcing my friends to stare with pained expressions, run fingers around the lips of cups, clear phlegm from their throats. It was like arriving at Lexi's, holding it all in at first, putting on a brave face. But unlike Lexi, Amy and Ted didn't seem inclined to giving me the chance to let it all out. I couldn't cry in front of them, or rant, or tell them how I felt. They didn't ask—or if they did, I could tell they hoped I wouldn't say too much. Perhaps they thought that the subject was taboo, and they simply were trying to respect my private grief.

I watched the two of them, and saw that they were as oblivious to the minutiae of married life as I once had been. Ted wandered around looking for his keys, then asked Amy if she had the number for their friend Max, and Amy answered that it was in the blue book, where it always was, and didn't Ted have it memorized by now? Amy washed dishes by hand and Ted dried them, a silent, easygoing routine interrupted now and then by an offhand comment. They fit together, a matched pair, like any couple—if you spied them separately, on the street, you might not put them together, but once you saw them interacting, it would seem a foregone conclusion. They smiled at each other, grazed each other crossing a room, handed each other a cup, a pen, the phone. It was no one thing, but the accumulation of a million things.

When I first met Amy and Ted, Dill and I had been married just six months. Ted had worked with Dill on a project, and the two of them played tennis and racquetball. When the four of us went out for dinner, Amy and I made a pointed effort to become friends, too, understanding that it was what was expected, the couples merging. While I sat across the table from Amy, I noticed how the candlelight glowed on her bare arm. She was thin and athletic, and wore a sundress with tiny ribbon straps. I was thinking I had worn the wrong thing, but then she smiled at me in a way that I understood she, too, was shy at first meetings. And since at first the only thing we had in common seemed to be our husbands' friendship, we started talking about our respective weddings. Amy's family, old-moneyed from the automobile industry, had thrown an enormous bash at a country club outside Detroit. It cost more than our house had, but I didn't dare comment. Amy's point of the story, however, was that she hated every minute of the reception, couldn't wait to get away from her parents and their friends and be alone with Ted.

"I wish we'd eloped," she said morosely.

"We did," I said.

Her eyes widened. "No kidding? I didn't know that! Where?"

"We just went to city hall one Friday afternoon during a blizzard and did it. We had been planning the wedding, but our hearts weren't in it. Both our dads had died, and Dill's mother hated to fly, and the more we thought about it, the more we just had to do it. *Now.*" I laughed.

"That is so romantic." Amy sighed. "I'm so jealous. Maybe I'll burn our wedding photos and just pretend that's what we did. It sounds perfect."

The day Dill and I got married, a sunny January turned into a swirling snowstorm by late afternoon. It got dark so early then, and on the way to city hall immense flakes spun around the streetlights and covered our heads like lace. We held hands so tightly it hurt, and that made us laugh, though neither of us let go. A puddle formed around our boots on the linoleum while we waited. The man who married us was called Dwayne VanDam; it was on a name tag pinned crookedly to his lapel, and while he spoke I kept wanting to straighten the tag. I did not hear what he said, except the part that mattered: Did I take Dillard Anthony Rainey as my lawful wedded husband? I did. We exchanged rings that had cost less than a hundred dollars each but matched. The gold felt cold on my finger but quickly warmed as if it had been there always, melted to my skin. We kissed. We grinned. Dwayne signed the license and so did his secretary, who smiled metallically, the surprise of a mouthful of kid's braces in a fifty-year-old face. "So," said Dill, my newly minted husband. "What do you want to do now?"

Amy was right. It was perfect.

On my second night, I made my shadowy way from the bathroom to guest room and heard them whispering in their doorway. Amy was pressed against Ted's wide chest, and she was gazing earnestly into his face, a soap opera couple. It almost made me laugh, but then I noticed tears lining her smooth cheekbones and I thought, I wonder if they've had some bad news, too. But then I could hear Amy saying, "It's just so sad. It kills me to be around her." Ted murmured, "I know." Then Amy: "It makes you realize how fragile life really is." Ted: "I know." Amy paused to weep a little while Ted stroked her hair like a cat's, smoothing it back from brow to nape. Amy looked again into her husband's eyes. "I just want you to know how much I love you. If nothing else, at least this makes me realize that *we are so lucky*." Ted said nothing but tilted down to cover Amy's mouth with his. I felt my feet sliding slowly toward my room; when I finally made it I closed the door silently behind me and stood there, shaking.

The next evening Ted asked how I was holding up, not looking at me, and I lied that I was fine. He clicked the remote, and we watched the kaleidoscope of channels until the three of us were hypnotized. One of the dogs yawned and the other burrowed underneath the coffee table. I thought about how Dill liked to watch television in the evenings, just to let the scenery slosh past, until he fell into a deeply bored but contented stupor. Sometimes I joined him, asking about the movie he seemed so engrossed in, though it became clear he simply had tired of switching channels and landed there, as oblivious as I to the plotlines. But he would sling an arm around my shoulder and mutter, "I'm not sure. Let's just watch."

When Ted paused for a long moment on a news channel, Amy and I grew alert, like children waiting to be told a story. The local game commission was considering a request by hunters to allow them to shoot mourning doves, because, according to an affable spokesman in camouflage, "It's really fun and challenging to try to shoot them, what with their erratic flying patterns." The birds swirled and dipped on-screen with a kind of sad elegance.

"Isn't there anything else, Ted?" Amy asked impatiently.

"Not really," he said, clicking.

We sat back and watched the colors whirl past, snippets of music, preaching, violence, mourning doves, used cars, and cat litter.

I finished my extended leave of absence from work, having used up all of my vacation and sick leave time, though my boss, Jillian, assured me "no one is counting." I worked as academic director for Upward Bound, a program designed to guide high-school students with borderline grades and no college graduates in their families toward higher education. Each teenager was paired with a college student on campus for tutoring in various subjects, while I counseled and offered practical advice on how to approach entrance exams, financial aid institutions, and college curricula. We had a small staff, only four people, and while in my grief I considered not returning at all, I also was guilt-ridden that the others had shifted my workload among them for so long. Yet, when I arrived on a Tuesday morning, late, my coworkers greeted me warmly.

"You're back!" Jeremy, the assistant director, exclaimed, then cleared his throat. "I'm so sorry," he said soberly. I nodded. He'd said the same thing at the funeral, and later, in a phone message at my mother's house.

"Anna," said Natalie, the receptionist, hugging me. She said nothing more and I appreciated that. She pushed her hair out of her face, smiled, and went back to her desk.

"So," Jillian, the program director, said, a comradely arm around my shoulder, "are you sure you should be here?"

"Yes. Sure," I said, wondering for a split second if she meant here, among the living, or here, in this office. I went to my little cubby with its blue-gray walls and navy chair, stacks of college brochures, admissions forms, and the copies of Carson McCullers's books I liked to hand out to students who claimed they hated reading. All I had to say to some sixteen-year-old girl was, "Here, she wrote this when she was twenty-three, and no one could believe someone so young could be so insightful," and she would take it from my hands with a look of thinly veiled curiosity. One thing I know about kids is this: They appreciate it when adults acknowledge their intelligence. They know everything, after all.

Sitting at my desk, I pretended to rearrange files for a while. I'd heard somewhere that you should carry on with normal tasks, even if your heart isn't in it. Eventually the very act of working—or eating or folding a towel or sifting potting soil—will move you and help you to wake up. I didn't feel awake yet, but I was moving. I could even sometimes notice that my stomach was growling or that I was frustrated or irritated (sensations other than torpor and exhaustion), and I supposed those were good signs. I also was surprised at how glad I was to be back at work. Mostly, I had missed the students. I wanted to hear their gossip, watch them air-box each other, flip each other's braids. By three o'clock I eagerly anticipated their arrival from school for their tutoring sessions. When they saw me, they stopped in a herd and stared wide-eyed.

Finally, Martin, a wiry runner, spoke up. "Hey, Miss Rainey, how're you doing?"

"Pretty good, considering," I said, smiling. I was touched that he'd asked. I felt so old all of a sudden; around the students I used to feel almost like a peer. Once, a seventeen-year-old named Marissa had asked me how old I was, and when I told her thirty-four, she'd gasped. "That's the same age as my mother!" she'd said. I had met her mother, a tired-looking woman with dyed auburn hair and rosacea, and I have to admit I was shocked by the comparison. Then Marissa had added kindly, "But *you* sure don't look it."

I decided I didn't want to stand there with them staring at me with pity and discomfort, so I just shrugged and said, "Hey, things just happen sometimes, you know." Then I dug into my pocket and pulled out a handful of quarters. "Drinks are on me today." I passed around the change and watched their faces brighten.

They sauntered toward the soda machine at the end of the hallway, tossing coins in the air and singing, "Heads. Tails."

I was back among the living, whether I was ready or not.

My former next-door neighbor, Gwen, tracked me down through first my mother and then Lexi, who left word with Amy that the mailman had stopped delivering to my house once he realized "what had happened." He had a boxful waiting at the post office for me, whenever I was ready to claim it.

I sat in my car in the parking lot, trying to muster the strength to open my door and walk inside. I could see people coming and going, lost in their thoughts and mundane tasks of dropping letters into a mailbox or carrying packages under one arm while holding the hand of a small, slow-moving child. Perhaps there was a woman in the lobby opening her silver box with a tiny key and pulling out a love letter, or a man mailing his dead father's watch to his brother; perhaps there were others for whom a visit to the post office meant something, shifting their lives in one direction or another.

For twenty minutes I sat in my front seat, listening to Vivaldi and Tchaikovsky on Classic 101.4 and running my fingers around the steering wheel, waiting for the right moment, a surge of courage, a divine nudge telling me I could do this. I could open a pile of letters and bills addressed to Dill Rainey, look at his name printed on a magazine label, think about him sitting at the kitchen table reading the "Harper's Index" aloud to me, find his reminder from the dentist noting that he was due for his six-month cleaning, open the checks from clients with scribbled notes saying, "Thanks, Dill! We loved the galleys—call me later this week to set up another meeting." I could do that; as the postman had said, I could "claim it."

Or, I could drive away.

I drove home, nearly. Out of deeply ingrained habit, like a migrating bird, I was within three blocks of my old house before I realized what I was doing. I had to stop the car on the side of the road to compose myself.

Just the night before, Ted had asked me gently if I wanted to go home to "retrieve some things," and I said no, thank you. He looked at me for a moment, then said, "Okay, then." I wondered for a few minutes after he left the room if he had begun resenting my daily consumption of his and Amy's food, soap, shampoo, and if I should have taken the hint. Or perhaps he was suggesting that I should go back, that it would be helpful to see my old house and Dill's things, as a kind of catharsis. It could have been a simple, innocent question; I wanted to ask him, then, what he *had* meant. After a while, though, I wearied of analyzing his comment and went off to take a long soak in the bathtub, careful not to use too much orange-scented oil.

As I turned my car around in an abrupt U-turn, I decided I just needed to retrain myself, learn new landmarks on the way to Amy and Ted's, so that I would not make the same mistake twice. Even though I knew my way to their house, I noted anew the graceful birches on the corner lot at the end of their long block; the stucco house with the gray trim and Peter Pan windows in the attic; the twin brick houses designed by the same architect some fifty years earlier; and then the cluster of Japanese maples ringing Amy and Ted's driveway. I had been here dozens of times before, for dinner with Dill and our friends, for their annual Christmas party (which, I realized, I had missed. Did I receive an invitation when I was at my mother's house? I couldn't recall), and sometimes just to drop in on a Saturday when the guys wanted to watch sports together. Amy and I would retreat to the kitchen to talk and eat all the dip and drink too many daiquiris. It occurred to me that, since I had moved in with them, Amy and I never sat alone and talked; she was always with Ted in their room, or the three of us were together eating, or watching television, as if we didn't know what else to do. She never made daiquiris now.

When I got to their house, they were already eating dinner, takeout deli food, and were laughing at something, unaware that I had arrived. As soon as they saw me, they both looked guilty, fussing over the packages on the table, getting up to set a place for me.

"No, it's okay," I said brightly. "Just go on, I already ate on my way home. I had to run some errands and just grabbed a burger. Thanks, anyway."

"You sure?" Ted asked.

"Yeah."

"How was your day?" Amy asked earnestly, as she did every day, as if I were their child returning from school. The quiet, moody child, drifting in and out.

I shrugged. "Fine. Good." I smiled and started upstairs, listening as they gradually resumed their intimate conversation. In the guest room, I lay down on the bed and inhaled the now-familiar scent of fabric softener on the sheets. I looked around the room. There was the flowered chaise, the shelves lined with spines of books I had memorized, and the blue lusterware planter I'd accidentally dropped my first night there, Amy rushing to tell me it was no big deal, though I could tell by her expression that it had been a prized possession. As a sign of goodwill, apparently, she later returned the glued-together piece to my room. She was generous with her clothes, too, insisting I borrow anything I wanted. On the back of the door hung one of Amy's robes I wore each morning from my room to the bathroom. One morning I'd run into Ted in his boxers, and he started to grab hold of my arm, then let go, laughing as he realized I wasn't his wife. "The robe," he said, blushing.

"Oh, sorry," I replied automatically, as if I had taken something I shouldn't have, though I knew Amy had other robes.

As I got up from the bed and started packing, I held the robe in my hands for a long moment. It was a slippery pale lavender satin, with a sash at the waist and perfect piping along the shawl collar. A more beautiful piece of lingerie than I had ever owned. At home I always wore flannel, or Dill's white terry-cloth robe that made me feel like a child in a snowsuit, so swaddled and bulky. Amy's robe was like liquid fabric, and in it I felt elegant, lovely. I couldn't help myself; I rolled it up and tucked it into my duffel bag and zipped away the evidence.

I left in the morning, on my way to work, telling Amy and Ted good-bye as if it were any other day, taking satisfaction in knowing that they would return to find my thank-you note and pile of sheets removed from the guest bed, and that they would sigh deeply, alone at last. In a week or so, I would sent them a gift, a tall ficus plant, or a beautiful piece of pottery, though I knew I could never properly repay them. Nor would I let myself grow so comfortable again in one place. I decided henceforth on a three-day rule.

I moved in with Philip, an old friend with whom I'd once worked in college admissions. He was offered a job in the alumni office but decided to stay put, joking that he preferred being at the bottom of the academic food chain. Philip and I had stayed in touch sporadically after I left to work for Upward Bound, since my office was still on campus, but less often after Dill and I got married. After I left Amy and Ted's, I knew Philip was the friend I needed. Rather than tiptoeing around my malaise, he would likely dive right in—and not solicitously like Lexi, but like a big, wet dog, wagging and sputtering and trying to make me laugh.

Back when Philip and I had shared a cubicle, phoning prospective students and raving about all the school had to offer, we would cross our eyes at each other and surreptitiously eat candy. We had discovered that it was possible to hold Hershey's Kisses tucked in the backs of our mouths and suck on them, all the while chatting away about the merits of a liberal arts education. The chocolate would begin to ooze between our teeth, and the game was to see which of us could successfully complete our spiel without actually swallowing the candy or drooling.

Philip was kind and irreverent, and believed in facing up to reality. "You know, chickens commit suicide more than any other farm animal," he informed me one morning while cracking eggs into a bowl, after I had been with him two days.

I stirred my coffee and said, "Oh, really?"

"Yeah," he said. "Why else do you think they're always crossing the road?" I laughed out loud for the first time in weeks, maybe months.

I was settling in, already breaking my new three-day rule. I couldn't resist, and besides, it was easier since we were both single; I wasn't interrupting the cadence of married life. We each talked about our days at work while Philip sautéed vegetables and stirred risotto, and then we would move to the living room to play Hard Scrabble, Philip's irreverent version, in which we could spell only naughty words or slang, a feat more difficult than it sounds. You think you know every bad word in the book, but given a dearth of vowels, you might come up with only *dip*. Philip kept careful track of the score (the more profane the word, the more likely the bonus points), but I noticed he often made room for me to nab the triple-point squares. Then, around ten-thirty, he would help me unfold the sofa bed, pat me on the head, and say, "Good night, John-boy," and sometimes all the other names of the Waltons, as he drifted down the hallway to his own room. I lay in the middle of the dark living room, set adrift on my foam bed, with Philip's cat, Prince Charles, thumping his tail on my leg till I fell asleep.

I liked the steady predictability of my days there; Philip and I had fallen into the rhythm of old chums, and he said nothing about my moving out. He said nothing about Dill, either, as I'd expected. It seemed he had grown more sensitive antennae, and a protective air like a big brother. I wasn't completely sure I liked this new side; I'd braced myself for his edgy humor, a good-natured assault on my moodiness, but he refrained.

Instead, he complimented my clothing when I left for work, and once told me he liked my robe. "It's very Grace Kellyish," he said. I looked down at the stolen robe and tied the sash a little tighter. "Thanks," I said. I'd thought about dropping it off at Amy's doorstep with an apologetic note, but I already had stained it with butter one morning, so it was too late. When I walked away from Philip to head to the bathroom, he whistled, and I laughed. His flirtations, feigned though they seemed, helped lift me enough to get me out the door each day.

My mother phoned me at work and asked tactfully, in a bright voice, if I was "living with someone."

"Well, for the time being," I said. "My friend, Philip."

"Oh. Do I know him?"

"Yes, we used to work together, remember? Tall, very amiable, funny. You know Philip, Mom, you used to love him."

"Oh, right," she said slowly. "He's cute." And then I realized what she was getting at.

"Mom, we're just friends. Honestly. I've been staying with friends lately. You know, I just need some company and Philip has plenty of room. I sleep on the sofa."

"A foldout?" she asked. "That's terrible for your back, you know."

"It's fine, Mom. It's temporary. But thank you for asking." I hung up before she could delve any deeper into her own suspicions.

One evening after work I arrived at Philip's before he did, and wandered into the kitchen to find Prince Charles terrorizing a mouse. Instinctively I grabbed a broom and swished the cat out of the way. Then I nudged the dust ball of a mouse toward the back door. Instead of taking advantage of my heroics, however, the mouse ran the other way, back toward the stove and through a crevice. Charles followed, wedging his fat, hairy body between the stove and the wall. The harder I pulled at him, the more hysterical the cat became. Finally I

29

shoved the stove with all my weight and dislodged him. He backed away, hindquarters raised as if preparing to attack me, so I grabbed the broom again in defense. I was startled by my sudden hostility, and my hand holding the broom handle shook.

Philip opened the front door and sang out, "Lucy, I'm home," in his best Ricky Ricardo accent. Prince Charles darted between Philip's legs and hid there, eyeing me.

"What are you doing?" Philip asked, tossing his keys onto the counter and shaking his curly hair like a dog. For a moment, I couldn't stop watching him—the way he hunched out of his coat and smoothed away the droplets of wet snow from his face. He reminded me of Dill, and I was startled. Philip and Dill were nothing alike, not in personality, body type, or fashion sense. Where Dill had been lean, blond, wearing tired sweaters and flannel shirts, Philip was tall, imposing, dark and theatrical. He wore nicely draping trousers and favored turtlenecks. He once said he always wanted to be a bohemian artist, except that he didn't have talent, or a Parisian bookseller, except that he didn't speak French. I told him he looked like something in between, and he almost blushed at the compliment.

When I set the broom down and explained what had happened, Philip smirked. "Well, I hate to tell you, but it's what cats do."

"Very funny," I said, and skulked off to burrow into the sofa. For once, the cat didn't follow. Philip came in to ask if I was all right. When I muttered, "I'm *fine*," my tone must have scared him off, too. I hoarded the remote control and watched television for four straight hours without moving. Philip brought me dinner, set it silently on the coffee table, and left without another word. I heard him washing dishes, sifting dry cat food into a metal dish, opening the back door to set out the trash. He kept busy, he stayed out of my way. He stopped in the living room only once more, to say, "Good night."

With my face pressed against a corduroy pillow, I lay still, listening to Philip's steady breathing in the next room while he slept, with his door ajar, and for the first time I considered the word *widow*. "I am a widow," I whispered to myself. I felt the abandonment of the word as I listened intently to Philip's snores.

In the middle of the night, I felt my way toward the kitchen for some water, and when I got there, in my bare feet, I stepped on something soft. Flicking on the light, I saw the mouse I had tried to rescue lying torn and mutilated on the linoleum. I stepped out of the way and screamed. Just a moment lapsed before Philip bolted into the room, blinking hard. "What? What's wrong?"

"I killed it."

When I pointed, he looked down at the tiny body and the flecks of blood. "Jeez. It looks like something Prince Charles would do." Philip seemed slightly dazed, trying to wake up.

"No, I mean, I tried to save him but I couldn't get him out, he was too far back behind the stove. He must have tried to creep out after dark and that damn cat got him anyway—"

"Wait a minute, wait a minute," Philip said. He was alert now. "It happens all the time. I hate to tell you how many of these little guys I've had to dump in the garden. It's no big deal. Really."

"My gosh, I hate him," I said. "I really hate him." Philip looked at his felonious cat and then at me, bewildered. "Not him," I said, impatiently. "Dill."

"Do you want to talk about it?"

I shook my head. Philip was silent; I couldn't tell what he was thinking. His smooth forehead throbbed at the temples, the veins small cords that looked like they would vibrate if I reached out to touch them. I could not help noticing that; the moment was so sharp, everything seemed to bristle around me. The lights blinked and flickered.

The refrigerator hummed softly. The cat padded into the room to see what was happening. I leaned heavily against the countertop and waited for the earth to cave in. As Philip pulled me into his broad chest, his skin scented with sleep, I began to weep. When he kissed my forehead tenderly, his lips lingering, I knew I had to go.

The next morning I was up before Philip, sitting beside the folded-up sofa bed and my packed bags. When he wandered in to find me, he didn't look surprised. He also looked like he hadn't slept at all. I realized then that, after he went back to his room, I hadn't heard any snoring.

"So where are you going—home?" he asked gently.

"No, not there," I said quickly. "I'm going to Lydia's."

Philip stood looking at me for a long moment, as if trying to decide whether or not to let me leave, then he carried my duffel bags out to my car and drove me across town himself. He said he would walk home; he liked the air this time of year. We said nothing on the way over, just watched our breath swirl in little clouds in front of our faces until it became a contest, to see which of us could blow the biggest puffs of air. By the time we arrived at Lydia's house, the windshield was completely fogged over.

"Well, here we are. Tell Lydia I said hello," Philip said. Lydia was my old college roommate Philip had once had a crush on, till he discovered how flaky she was. He still liked her, though, he'd once told me, in a "lusty stepbrother kind of way." One thing I could say about Philip was that he had an uncanny instinct about the right way to respond to situations. He never vacillated once he made a decision, and he never apologized. I admired that.

I knew you would call," Lydia said as soon as I was in her apartment. "I just had a feeling." Lydia was wearing dangling teapot earrings and overalls covered with tiny pink flecks of what appeared to be tissue. She explained that she was working on a mixed-media piece. She told me it was a perfect time for me to move in with her because she had just broken up with a long-term boyfriend and, like me, needed a female friend to regain her perspective. "Not that it is anything like what you are going through," she added apologetically.

I said, "Everyone has their problems."

"That's true," she murmured.

No one who hasn't been through it can imagine. "I can't imagine what you're going through," they say. Of course they can't. But I could tell them that you'd be amazed to find what you can do, in spite of it all. You can get up each day and shower, squirting the dollop of shampoo into your palm, noting or not noting the herbal scent; pick out clothes (is it warm or cool? short sleeves or cardigan? socks or no?) and put them on. You watch the coffee drip and sizzle from the filter, then pour it mindlessly into your cup, sensing or not sensing the hard porcelain against your lip as you drink. You can gather keys and walk outside and drive to your job, and smile at your colleagues sympathetically when one tells you his dog is sick with heartworm, another that her husband is cranky. You decide what to eat for lunch and eat it, and all the while, you know in some barely sealed room of your heart that you are utterly alone in the world. You think, *He's dead, he's dead, he's dead*, a hypnotizing and terrifying mantra, even as you reach for more mayonnaise for your turkey sandwich and sip your iced tea wishing the waiter had put in more ice. You do what you have to do, and if you are lucky, you have friends around to distract you, if nothing else.

Like the others, Lydia was gracious, though perhaps more cheerfully so; also, more time had lapsed—whole months, somehow—and my wounds weren't so fresh or off-putting. After a few days, Lydia seemed to forget that the reason for my newly single status was different from hers and said we just needed to have some "good old-fashioned girl time," as if it were an extended slumber party.

Lydia reminded me of my childhood best friend who lived next door. Kara had her own room, like mine, except that hers was pink-carpeted and lined, wall to wall, with Barbie paraphernalia. She had the Dream House, the Jeep, camper, beauty salon, powerboat, and horses. She also owned every one of Barbie's various girlfriends, in every color from deep brown to golden to rosy Caucasian, all of them the same age and height except for Skipper, the adoring little sister. Kara had one Ken, dressed in a casual sweater and jeans, with his level gaze and placid smile.

"The girls," as we called them, gathered together to plan their parties and dates and discuss the War. The War was where most of the imaginary men had been banished; when we tired of solo Ken as the rotating date for all of the dolls, and we didn't know what to do with him, we sent him "over there." Sometimes we pretended he had just been in a terrible car accident and Barbie visited him in the hospital, lovingly bent over his flat bed and kissed him. We had to cover his face with a tiny torn piece of towel because his bright eyes and constant smile belied his injuries. Most of the time, though, we simply shoved Ken under the dust ruffle of Kara's bed and had the girls talk about how awful the War was and how Ken had been wounded but wrote every day. It was easier that way, playing with the women we knew best, projecting onto them our small desires and conversations, without the complicated interference of the male species, about which we knew so little. At nine, we thought girlfriends were all we could possibly want or need in life, never suspecting that when we got older we would prefer to be alone with our Kens, day after day, night after night, and then never suspecting that life could thrust us backward to that time when it was just "the girls."

So there I was, huddled over wine and nail polish, putting on my game face, pretending to be content with the scenario. Lydia's apartment was small, the top floor of an old house, with only one bed, but she loaned me her "guest nook," which had a huge brown velvet pillow on the floor like a giant pincushion, or a cat's bed. She also generously supplied extra clothes and a crystal to hang around my neck. Lydia was a firm believer in "everything, whatever it takes." Prayer, horoscopes, candlelight, saints, organic food, vodka, whole grains, and even cocoa. I ate a lot of brownies.

Y ou're not so skinny now," Martin informed me one afternoon. His tutor was having a root canal, so I was filling in, trying to go over a list of vocabulary words with him.

"Thanks. I guess," I said.

"It was a compliment," Martin said. "You were way too skinny before. Girls always look better with some flesh on 'em. Women, too," he amended, smiling.

"Okay, let's get back to the subject here, Romeo," I said, pointing to the third word on his list. *"Reciprocity."*

"What about it?"

I sighed. "Define it, please."

He leaned back in his chair, fiddled with the zipper of his jacket. Up, down, zip, zip. He stared at the ceiling. Finally, as I opened my mouth to prompt him, he chanted, "Reciprocity is my name, returning favors is my game, you do your thing, and I do mine, and maybe we get along just fine."

"Very nice," I said. "Have you been working on that or did you just make it up?"

Martin shrugged. "Made it up. I can do it in my sleep. This one just came to me because I remembered the 'favor' part. I looked it up." He smiled a little.

"That's impressive, "I said. "Ready for the next word? Or do you need a moment to compose?" Martin gave me a look. "Okay," I said, *"incidentally."*

"Don't know it. Give me a hint."

"Think of the root—*incidental.* Or *incident.*"

"Oh, that helps a lot," he said sarcastically.

"Do you want me just to tell you the definition?" I asked. I was suddenly tired. It seemed like too much work to placate someone else. I wanted to go home to Philip's and lie down while he cooked me dinner. Then I remembered that I wasn't living there anymore; I was living with Lydia, where lying down was nearly impossible. I had to curl into a ball and wake feeling stiff and unsettled. I sat back and watched Martin zip and unzip his jacket some more, and it occurred to me that it actually was rather soothing, that I could probably sit and listen to it all day. The Zen of zippers. I suddenly laughed.

"What's so funny?"

"Nothing," I said, laughing some more. "I don't know. Everything, sometimes." I stopped laughing and said, "*Incidentally,* this could be a sign of a nervous breakdown." My student looked worried. He leaned up and peered around the open doorway as if hoping help was on the way. "Never mind," I said. "Listen, why don't you look up the words you don't know and write a sentence using each one?"

Martin groaned. I knew that the command to write almost always elicited protest if not disgust from the kids. But I also knew that it almost always arose from a lack of experience and practice. The more they wrote, and read, and figured things out, the more confident they would become.

"Here, use this. It might help," I told Martin, handing him Strunk and White's *The Elements of Style.* I knew Martin had a tendency to ramble in his writing, to misuse words or tangle his syntax. Like many students, he hated grammar and spelling rules, the annoying inconsistencies—*i* before *e* except after *c*—and illogical pronunciations.

Martin took the tiny book, opened to a random page, and read aloud in a monotone, " 'Use a colon after an independent clause to introduce a list of particulars, an appositive, an amplification, or an illustrative quotation.' Yeah, that's helpful." He laughed.

"Okay, okay," I said. "Just think of some original sentences and I'll be right back."

I suddenly needed a moment alone. I pushed the dictionary across the table along with a legal pad and pen, and left the room. I walked down the hall, past the soda machine and to the exit. Outside, I took a deep breath. Snow had melted the night before, a fluke February thaw, as if spring had decided to pop up early. But now it had frozen hard again, and icicles had sprouted from every overhang, even the fender of a parked car, like a row of tiny fangs. I liked the cold snap of the air, and I was tempted to keep walking. Instead I continued standing against the outside wall of my familiar building, with familiar colleagues and students inside, working away on their little tasks. Martin, I was sure, in spite of his reluctance, was busy flipping through the dictionary in an effort to get his work over with. I envied him the pettiness of his responsibilities, the fact that what mattered was passing English and breaking school track records, and getting girls to look at him, and composing rap songs in his head. I wished I were a confident fifteen-year-old boy, tapping out poems, instead of being a disconnected grown woman, a grieving widow. *I know this lady/her husband has died/she lives with friends and thinks of suicide.* Of course, I didn't really think about suicide. I just thought about sleeping.

When I went back to my office, Martin was gone. On the table he had left his paper with the sentences in loopy cursive:

> *Incidentally,* the ink ran out of my pen. Oh, here's a pencil.
>
> My teacher likes to *exhort* me to work hard.
>
> I run with *insouciance.*
>
> *Gratify* rymes [*sic*] with *satisfy.*

When I went into the hallway, I found the other students gathering book bags and jackets and preparing to leave. It was five o'clock, the daylight waning. Time really flew at work, I'd discovered.

"Where's Martin?" I asked Sheena, the girl nearest the exit.

She shrugged. "He got a phone call and then he left."

No one else claimed to know anything, so I went to talk to the secretary. Natalie looked up from behind her square tortoiseshell glasses and raised her thin brows. "His mother called. Apparently Martin's younger brother was in an accident. I tried to find you, but you must have been in the ladies' room."

I stood there, stunned. Maybe if I hadn't left Martin alone, this wouldn't have happened. Maybe I was bad luck.

"Is he okay?" I said finally. "His brother?"

"I don't know, she didn't say, she just asked if Martin was here and could we send him straight home. I think someone was going to drive him to the hospital."

The hospital. I hadn't been there since Dill died. I had the compulsive urge to intercept Martin on the way there, to warn him that it was no place for his brother, that no one got out of there alive. But I knew I couldn't say those things. And maybe they weren't even true; I had no perspective.

"I have to go," I told Natalie. "Tell Jillian for me, okay?"

I didn't go to the hospital, though. I couldn't. I went back to Lydia's apartment, which, fortunately, was empty. Lydia, I remembered, was attending a friend's opening at a local gallery. I threw my coat and gloves onto a chair and started pacing. Life wasn't supposed to be like this; children were supposed to live, couples were supposed to marry and grow old together, people were supposed to find their niches and then fill them. I was wandering around, cut loose, every day some new obstacle thrown into my pathway for me to trip over, dig around, or try to surmount.

I went into the bathroom to hunt for some aspirin to quiet the pounding in my head. When I opened Lydia's medicine cabinet, I felt a wash of déjà vu.

Suddenly, I was twenty-eight, standing in my own apartment, getting ready to meet Dill for dinner. We had been dating for three months, and were taking it slowly—almost too slowly for me. We kissed endlessly at the end of dates, and Dill knew where to touch and how much, but he never went too far. A perfect gentleman. Still. I'd stood in front of my little medicine cabinet fingering a compact of birth control pills. Every day I opened it and pressed one free from the foil nest. A superstitious part of me thought I might be jinxing our romance by planning ahead. On the other hand, I didn't want to wind up entangled one night, watching Dill emerge breathless from the sheets to hunt for a condom. I had done that before, with others, and a part of me deflated inside at the desperation of a man's desire, my sometimes merely incidental part in the process. But now it was different. I was in love. I didn't know why Dill was waiting, but I wasn't sure I could stand waiting anymore.

I waited in a tight sweater with belled sleeves, a skirt, and black boots. The doorbell finally rang, and I pressed the intercom, listened to Dill blowing into the speaker to sound like the wind. Then he was there, standing in my doorway with a lopsided grin.

He held out two hands. "Choose one," he said, still smiling. I pointed to the left. A stick of gum.

"Thanks," I said, and laughed.

"Try again," he said, shaking the other fist a little. I pointed, and his fingers uncurled slowly as a snail, revealing a tiny diamond ring in his flattened palm. I was too flabbergasted to speak. When I finally pulled him inside, we barely made it to the sofa before we were half undressed. We made love then on the flokati rug, the long strands of wool lapping at my bare legs. Afterward he said he had been holding out because it seemed too good to be true and hadn't wanted to ruin anything.

"So, did we?" I asked.

"No," he said, smiling at me. "So far, so good."

Four months later we were married in a blizzard, holding hands at city hall, promising each other our "troths." *Until death us do part.*

In Lydia's bathroom, I suddenly turned and retched into the toilet. I had thought that after time I would stop remembering the details. I didn't want the details, didn't want to be tormented by what was and what was gone. I didn't want to see him anymore.

"He isn't coming back," a small voice said, and I turned, wiping my mouth, to see where it came from. Then I realized it was my own.

In the silence of the apartment, my own thoughts seemed to echo.

"I'm home!" someone else called. It was Lydia. I hurriedly rinsed my mouth and shoved back my hair, found a composed expression and pasted it on, emerging from the bathroom as if nothing were out of the ordinary. I wondered if Lydia could sense it, being telepathic, but for once, she seemed oblivious.

"How was your day?" she asked, unloading a small brown bag of groceries onto her counter.

"Fine," I said, coming to sit nearby, at the table. "Need help?"

"No, it's just a few things for breakfast. Did you eat dinner, by the way?"

I knew it was Lydia's way of checking up on me, making sure I was taking care of myself. I had seen her opening a leftover container of vegetarian lasagna one night to see if any had been eaten, after she'd insisted I help myself.

"I had a little snack on campus. I wasn't that hungry," I said, adding as if by way of explanation, "One of my students has a brother who was in a car accident."

"Oh, no!" Lydia said, turning to me. "Is it bad?"

"I don't know," I said, embarrassed. "I haven't even called yet. I guess I should go to the hospital and see him."

Lydia stopped sorting groceries and studied me. It was disconcerting when she did that, trying to read people's minds. She had such a strong empathetic streak, she often came close. "You don't want to go, do you?" she said.

I shook my head. "I'm horrible, right?"

"No, not at all," she said. She pulled a bottle of red wine from a cupboard and held it out. "Time for a drink," she said. I laughed. It was nice to have friends who were so supportive of my drowning my sorrows. When we finished our third glasses of Chianti, sitting on the floor pillows arranged around the coffee table, Lydia pushed her blond hair out of her eyes and blinked at me. Her eyes were very large and brown, and she favored false eyelashes. For a moment she reminded me of Clarisse, the doe who didn't mind Rudolph's red nose.

"If you were an animal," I said, "what would you want to be?"

"Why do you ask?" she laughed.

"I don't know, you look like a reindeer."

"You might be drunk, hon."

"No, I don't think so," I said. "I think I would be a bear, so I could hibernate."

"Hmm," said Lydia.

I scowled at her. "Are you going to start analyzing me?"

Lydia scooted over closer to me. "You just want to sleep all the time, don't you? That's perfectly normal, you know. It's okay." I put my head down on the coffee table. I moaned. Not this, I thought. I don't want to talk about this. "You need to talk about this," she said. "I know of this support group. For survivors of death."

I lifted my head. "That sounds like I crawled out of a plane crash or something. This isn't that dramatic, unfortunately. People die every day in horrible ways—plane crashes, murders, gruesome accidents." I said flatly, "My husband just died. End of story."

"No, it's not the end of the story," she said calmly, rubbing her hand down my spine. "Maybe talking about it with other people who have been through it would help."

What difference do our words make? I wondered. Nothing anyone could say would explain life and its confounding mysteries, its hellacious tricks.

The next morning I called the hospital, but they wouldn't tell me anything about Martin's brother. It didn't help that I didn't even know his first name. "Do you have any patient by the last name of Wallace?"

"We have two, actually," the receptionist said. "Which one, please."

"I'm not sure," I said helplessly. "It's a boy, I'm not sure how old—"

"We can't give any information out unless you are next of kin." Obviously I wasn't, so she hung up.

I called Natalie at the office to tell her I would be late and to ask for Martin's home phone number. I had to get involved; life wasn't all about me. Everyone has to find a cause, and Martin somehow had become mine. I wanted to let him know I was there if he needed me, though I had no idea what I could do to help under the circumstances.

Martin's nine-year-old brother, James, had a closed-head injury. The kind that could cause permanent brain damage, impair his physical or cognitive development, or quite contrarily, clear up in a few weeks and leave James "just as good as new," according to his mother, Angela. Even on the phone, I could hear her clinging to those words like a fistful of magic beans. I had had the same thoughts about Dill. He'll be fine! The doctors will fix him right up!

I had called to find out what had happened and offer my sympathy, prayers, the things people so generously had pressed upon me. Though we all knew it wasn't enough. Only turning back time would be enough.

Later, when I stopped by the hospital waiting room, Angela said as much. "I had a bad feeling, you know, about him riding home with

Jay. Because of the weather, I mean." Jay, I now knew, was a twenty-year-old neighbor. When Angela had to work late, Jay often drove James home after his basketball practice at the civic center. The roads were icy, though, from the thaw and then a cold snap. One thing always leads to another, I thought.

"I should've just left work early, to get him myself," Angela said, her voice breaking. She rubbed her eyes, then held her arms tightly around herself.

"It's not your fault," I said. I knew what a lie that was. Of course it was her fault, Jay's fault, the weatherman's fault—everything is our own damn fault, somehow. We make little slips, and the house of cards tumbles down.

"And Jay—poor thing," Angela was saying.

I was stunned by her lack of malice. Jay—after spinning his car out of control on a left turn, smashing into a two-hundred-year-old oak tree, and demolishing the car, which crushed the skull of little James—had walked away unscathed. Well, physically, anyway. Of course, I knew what she meant. It was almost worse for him. He would have to wake up every day thinking, What have I done?

"Is there anything I can do?" I asked softly.

Angela smiled wanly. "No, thank you for stopping by, though, it was thoughtful of you. I know Martin really thinks a lot of you." She hesitated. "And I'm so sorry about your husband."

I bit my lip hard enough to taste skin, blood. "Well, tell Martin I said hello. I'll talk to him later." Then I turned and walked as quickly as I could without running through the hospital exit.

Your mother called," Lydia said when I got home. "I think she's worried about you."

"Why?" I said, taking off my shoes and joining Lydia at the long dining table she never used for dining, only art. It was so covered in dabs and smears of paint and glue it looked almost organic, as if it had erupted or evolved out of her floor. Even the legs had tufts of dried paint and bits of rags all over them. It was hard to resist picking at them.

"Well, probably because she hasn't seen you in a month and she thought you were still with Philip, and got my number from him. I think maybe your mother worries that you're drifting."

"Am I?" I said. "Do you think I'm a drifter? I thought I was more like a squatter, you know, since I just moved in here and took over your cat bed."

Lydia looked at me over her canvas. So far it had one dinner-plate-size circle of orange with streams of blue coming from the sides. If I stared long enough at one of her paintings, it made me think of something, but I didn't immediately feel anything, except sometimes dizzy; Lydia was very fond of circles.

"It's not a cat bed," she said, but good-naturedly. "It's merely a round bed, for unity and tranquillity. Aren't you tranquil when you sleep on it?"

"It's fine, really, I was just kidding."

"Anyway, you know you're welcome here as long as you want to stay," Lydia said softly, dabbing more blue around the center. "I think Lexi is hurt you've stayed on here a lot longer than with her."

I was momentarily taken aback. "I just thought it was time to move on, I guess."

"I meant, you know, Lexi worried that Penny was a distraction, too much for you to deal with right now, a noisy kid running around all giddy and cheerful like kids are."

"That's what she thought? And when is she telling you all this stuff?"

"Don't be mad. We don't gossip. We just worry about you. It's what friends do."

"Well, everyone can just stop worrying and get on with their lives, okay? I'm fine." I thought about the aspirin again, and wondered how many it would take to calm the thunder in my head. I wondered for a moment—an unexpected rush of hope—whether I had what Dill had had, and would soon succumb to the same outcome. We would be buried side by side. I was surprised at how glad it made me feel. Then I felt panic instead. I cleared my throat and went to get myself some water. From across the room I watched Lydia painting. I envied her, like Martin, going about her simple life, developing God-given talents, working, loving life enough to paint from it or write about it, or to sing. All of those things demanded passion, attention, emotion.

I emptied my glass and refilled it, then let the water run over my hands, first scalding hot, then cold, back and forth. My hands turned red, but I kept rinsing them, not knowing if what compelled me was the sensation of water, the eventual numbness, or the quiet rushing of sound that I didn't want to end. If Lydia noticed, she said nothing.

M y mother wasn't inside, though I called and checked all the rooms; I had told her only fifteen minutes earlier that I was on my way over. Then I saw her through the sliding doors to the backyard. She was stooped over something in the grass. I walked to the glass for a closer look and saw that it was not one thing but many, and at first it looked as though she were surrounded by small children. She was, in a way—they were statuettes of children, at least a dozen of them. And numerous gnomes; two deer, one with bowed head, the other looking up; a few rabbits; a fairy; and a giant toad.

"Mom?" I called, sliding open the heavy door a few inches. "What exactly are you doing out here?"

She turned, pushed her huge glasses up on her nose, and smiled at me. "Oh, hi, honey! I didn't hear you drive up." She stood upright and flexed her back. "What do you think? Do you like them, my little friends?"

"Um, yeah, I guess," I said. Friends? I wondered what had brought on this peculiar indulgence. My mother had always enjoyed collecting, and she often flipped to the shopping network on television, raving aloud about the dolls, though, to my relief, she never ordered any, claiming they were overpriced. Yet here she had what must have represented hundreds of dollars in concrete and paint. She had transformed her backyard into a miniature Disneyland. Even the striped lawn chairs suddenly looked festive, cartoonish. In contrast, the hedgerow, the maple trees, and the creeping myrtle that surrounded the fence all looked out of place, too natural and subtle in their late-winter drab. The snow was gone, but the ground was cold and hard.

"Is this—permanent?" I asked, stepping out into the yard.

My mother laughed, bending to heave a red-capped gnome a few inches to the left, so that he faced his peers. "No, they're movable. It just takes a little muscle."

"No, I meant, are you keeping *all* of these?"

"Yes, of course. I bought them," she said simply. I wondered if she had mentioned this idea before, when I wasn't listening, which was often. Her voice was like white noise to me; I liked the sound of it, but I rarely paid attention to what she actually said, because she usually had nothing to say. She could prattle on about wallpaper patterns, clogged duct vents, the difference between strudel and streusel, and never come to any kind of conclusion whatsoever. When my father was alive, she seemed interested in real issues, in politics and poverty and education and cancer research. My father loved to talk, and the two of them could stay up all night after the news discussing the latest drama. It almost seemed that my mother's way of coping with the loss of her companion was to talk about things of no consequence, no depth. And though she used to have what I considered odd hobbies—sewing doll clothes, for instance, though I didn't play with dolls except at Kara's house—this was something new and more alarming.

"Mom," I said. "Let's go inside and have some coffee."

"Are you all right?" my mother asked me, settling down at her table while I sifted ground coffee into the paper filter. It was stiff and stained from overuse; my mother didn't believe in throwing anything away if one more use could be squeezed from it.

"I was going to ask you the same thing," I said, careful not to sound anxious, but interested.

"I'm fine, honey, just sick of winter. I wanted to spruce things up a little. Isn't it cheerful?" She smiled, waving an arm toward the glass door. Her stone children seemed to smile back at us.

"They're really cute, Mom, but you sure got a lot of them."

"You need a lot to make scenes, you know."

"Scenes?"

"Yes, like from a play or movie, only still, like a photograph. A tableau." My mother stood up and walked back to look outside, musing. I stared at her. Was my mother turning into some kind of performance artist? Or was it simply a harmless new pastime? What was wrong with someone wanting to arrange concrete characters in an imaginary pageant? Nothing, unless the person was sixty-one years old and your mother.

"Well, I should go," I said, turning the coffeepot on to drip.

"Already? But you didn't have any coffee yet," my mother said.

"I know. I guess I wasn't in the mood for it after all. I'm trying to cut back on caffeine."

"Anna, are you sure you're all right?" She paused. "Do you want to move back here? You can, you know. Anytime. We would love to have you around."

Suddenly I had the awful thought that by *we* my mother was no longer including my absent father out of habit but her newfound menagerie of statues. I was torn between wanting to sit her down and sort it all out, and wanting to put on my coat and walk away as if I had never seen any of this. As I pulled the door behind me, I promised to call. Soon.

L ydia listened sympathetically and then said, "Everyone thinks their mothers are half insane; it's a birthright."

"Yes, but you haven't seen her yard. You wouldn't believe it. And her glasses are so gigantic it's like her cheeks are nearsighted. I mean, everything about her seems off-kilter, and I don't know if she's always been this way and I just didn't notice, or if it just happened recently, since my dad died." I paused. "But that was nine years ago."

Lydia looked at me. She said nothing, but I could see her processing it all, withholding judgment. I wanted her to join in, to confirm or deny my suspicions, to tell me that I was right, my mother was crazy and, in a matter of time, I would be, too. But either Lydia couldn't say such things or they hadn't occurred to her. Sometimes

I thought Lydia was much simpler than she seemed, that her being an artist didn't mean there were great depths below her surface. Perhaps she was a grown-up child, someone who painted because she liked the pretty colors, and the attention she got for good work. Sometimes she did indeed seem surprised by it all, wandering through her gallery openings with a loopy grin. On the other hand, she was disarmingly insightful, genuinely well-meaning, and kind. Kindness, I knew, was nothing to sneeze at.

Lydia handed me the newspaper and the telephone, then discreetly left the room.

SOLO, Survivors of Lost Ones, was one of numerous listings in the "self-help" section of the newspaper. Among the others were Nicotine Anonymous ("brown bag lunch meeting"); Overeaters Anonymous; Alcoholics Anonymous at Our Lady of the Lake Rectory; Recovery, Inc. (for panic attacks, nervous ailments); Stepmothers Support Group; Anxiety Support Group; Codependency Support (which I thought sounded vaguely oxymoronic); Hope Keepers (for chronic pain sufferers); and D.A.D. (Depression After Delivery. I thought it odd the acronym was for the father rather than the mother, though who can argue that one suffers more than the other?). Lydia had circled SOLO helpfully, and I dialed the number, though the thought of talking about death with a bunch of other depressed, abandoned people terrified me. Once I showed up, I would be "in," and they would know my name, my story, and I would have to endure whatever came next. Not only that, Survivors of Lost Ones sounded to me like the aftermath of an alien abduction. But I called and wrote down the information for the next meeting on the margin of the newspaper.

On Tuesday night, Joanne, the group leader (or facilitator, as she said), led me to a table to fill out a SOLO name tag. I considered writing a pseudonym but took the black marker and wrote my own name in bold print. I didn't add my last name, which was Dill's; it occurred to me that I had avoided writing it since his death, as any tiny reminder was like another jolt of pain. It had been four and a half months.

We stood around, the group awaiting instructions, and finally Joanne invited us to sit down. There was a semicircle of plushly upholstered armchairs, and we sank into them gratefully, like cocoons. I noticed how each person had a way of curling up, sealing off the outer world— crossed legs and arms, cardigans double-wrapped over chests, hair hanging loosely. The last was my method; I was glad to have long hair, which Dill liked to lift up and say, "The curtain rises, the audience holds its breath." I let the curtain fall around me, protectively, my mind wandering while Joanne made gentle introductions. She described our purpose—to "find a common ground, make some connections, vent and rant if necessary, comfort each other, support one another, and little by little, find our way to the future." I thought it sounded a little scripted, her careful wording, and that finding my way to the future was not on my to-do list. I just wanted to be able to endure the present. I wondered if I should just say so—*vent and rant*—but I didn't really want to, not here, not with these people.

"I hope you will feel comfortable here, even if it takes a few weeks," Joanne said. "You just have to give it time and you will find it is worth it. It is worth the risk."

She invited everyone to sit silently for a few moments and then, if anyone wanted to speak, he or she should feel free to do so. During the silence, which felt strangely forced, like a time-out, I avoided looking at the others and thought about what I might say: that I didn't really want to be here, that no matter how much—or how little—we talked, nothing would change. Dill and all the other loved ones still would be dead, absent, and we still would be uselessly present, sad and alone. Solo.

"Okay," Joanne said softly. She looked around the circle at each of us and nodded as if to signal us to wake up and respond. No one did, for what seemed like an eternity. There were four women, three older than I, probably mid-fifties, and one who looked barely twenty, with a pink scar that ran the length of her calf, which was exposed. She was wearing a short denim skirt, in spite of the chilly weather, and battered Birkenstock sandals. There was only one man in the group, forty-ish, ashen, probably once handsome, twirling his wedding band and staring at the floor.

When Joanne cleared her throat, he spoke as if prodded. Without looking up, he blurted, "My wife had cancer for six years. Our daughter was four when we found out, and she had to watch her mother slip away from her almost her whole childhood. Now she lies in her bed at night, crying, and asking me, 'Why couldn't we keep her longer, why couldn't Mom just go on being sick, it wasn't that bad, Mom being quiet and tired. I didn't mind.' " He paused. "What do I say to that?"

I sat there stunned, picturing a ten-year-old girl, wan and motherless, lying in a flowered twin bed and weeping.

Joanne nodded at him, reached over and held his arm for a minute, then said, "It's hardest when a child is involved. You focus so much on her grief, you can't face your own. Maybe we can talk about how *you* are coping."

The man, whose name tag read "Jon Gordon, Jr.," adjusted his weight in his chair and scowled a little. "I'm not— I mean, I'm *coping*, what else can you do? But I have to think about Celie, you know? She's the most important thing."

"I know that, I know," Joanne said gently. "I just want you to think for a few minutes about how you are feeling about your wife's death, about not having her in your life for you, and then we can go from there." Jon Gordon, Jr., said nothing, just wrapped his arms around his middle and leaned over as if he might be sick. I had the urge to tell Joanne to lay off him, she'd utterly missed his point.

The Birkenstocks girl sighed heavily, as if she were watching a movie that bored her. When she noticed several people looking at her, she offered a posed, artificial smile, then turned away, her face blank again. Clearly, she had things to say but would not—or could not—say them.

Then a woman named Vera, whose twenty-year-old daughter had died in a car accident, gripped the arms of her chair and made watery eye contact with Joanne, or a spot just beyond Joanne. She seemed unfocused, like a person coming out of anesthesia, unsure of where she was or why her body was throbbing with pain. "I feel like glass," Vera said huskily. Her words were so clear and true, I felt tears well up in my own eyes, too, as if Vera and I were Siamese twins, sharing the same blood vessels and nerve endings. And we were both trying not to shatter.

Martin's brother, James, was moved into another wing of the hospital, the long-term-care unit. Although he was still in a coma, there was hope that with continual muscular therapy—massage, and the manipulation of his limbs, exercised for him by nurses—he would not atrophy, and by the time he "came to" he would be ready for rehabilitation. Angela told me all of this brightly when I phoned again.

She said, "I talk to him all the time, and Martin reads or sings to him, and I'm sure he's getting sick of us, because I know he hears. I just know it." I imagined Angela smiling on the other end of the receiver, so certain of the power of her love for her child, the magic touch of nurses, the rhythmic swooshing of the oxygen machines, the hidden Hand of God.

I delicately changed the subject. "I was wondering if Martin is planning to come to the summer program," I said. "I know how things have been— I just hope he still comes."

Angela sighed. "I don't know. I really need him here with me, and with James. Maybe he'll just have to skip this time."

"I see. I understand," I said. "Do you think he would like to come to the end-of-the-year party next month? At the skating rink?"

There was a pause on the line, during which I thought I could read Angela's mind. Skating is risky. Kids fall, they can hit their heads. I wanted to say: "It will be fine, you should see Martin on skates, he's so graceful, and careful. Sometimes he grabs the hands of the ones— usually girls—who aren't as steady. And there will be pizza, a harmless outing." But I didn't say that. There was no such thing as *harmless* in Angela Wallace's vocabulary anymore.

"We'll see," she said. "I better go now. James needs me." And she was gone. I thought of her sitting beside the bed of her sleeping boy, just as I had with Dill, wiping his brow, watching him lovingly, intensely, waiting for a sign. She would press a hand to his warm cheek, touch his temple, and wonder what he was dreaming about. Did he hear her—*Hello, hello, you in there?*—or was he lost in some faraway landscape, bits of information and words and memories floating like clouds through his sleepy consciousness? There was no way of knowing. Nor was there any way of knowing how it would end, though I knew how Angela felt, naively assuming he would just sit up one day and smile at her.

After work, I drove past Martin's house, knowing his mother wouldn't be there, camped as she was at James's bedside. But I thought Martin might be home; after all, he couldn't stay at the hospital all the time. It was too much to expect of a teenager, even if he loved his brother. My instincts were right. Martin was sitting on the top step of his front porch, hunched over something in his lap. When I parked and got out of my car, I walked toward him and could see the thing was a kitten, no bigger than a sponge.

"Wow. That looks brand new," I said.

"Hi, Miss Rainey," he said without looking up. His voice was low and soft, as though he weren't accustomed to conversation. He hadn't been back to Upward Bound since the accident, five weeks earlier. It was now early April, and purple crocuses lined the sidewalk leading to Martin's big shoes. Tentatively, I sat down beside him. I knew he had received the messages from me, and the notes from tutors wishing him well. He still attended school, I was relieved to learn, though one of the girls at the program noted that he was "there, but, like, not there, you know what I mean?" I did. I knew exactly what she meant.

"So, how are you, Martin?" I asked. He shrugged. "Is that a he or a she?"

"She," he said, lifting his hand a bit so the kitten's head poked from underneath it as if on a spring. "Her name's Kiki. You want to hold her?" I thought about how I despised Prince Charles, and that I never really was a cat person, but he handed the kitten over before I could respond, and so I took the weightless fluff onto my lap. Martin brushed his hands together, then tucked them underneath his armpits as if not sure what to do with them now that he had nothing to hold.

"Hi, Kiki," I said in a silly, high-pitched voice. Then I simply sat and ran my fingers over the kitten's gray back in short, slow motions, till I felt the body relax and the tiny hum under my palm. "I talked to your mother," I said to Martin, who merely nodded. "She says James is doing pretty well—"

"He's not," Martin blurted. He looked straight at me then, his eyes sorrowful. "He's practically *dead*, but my mom just keeps on sitting there and sitting there and talking to him like a crazy person. I tell her he can't hear her, but she gets so upset, I lie and say maybe he can. I just wish he would go on and die. It would be better."

"No," I said quickly. "It wouldn't be better, Martin. Even if it doesn't seem like it, there's still hope for James. People often recover from serious injuries, from comas. I promise you that if my husband were alive, even in a coma, I would be grateful. It has to be better than—gone." By the end, my voice had nearly vanished, so I was not sure that Martin heard me. But he reached over and touched my shoulder awkwardly, then took his hand away.

I cupped my hand around the kitten, fur tufting between my fingers. The tiny head butted against me like the soft ball of someone's foot nudging. I handed her back to Martin. "Do you think you can make it to the ceremony the end of May? I know your mother isn't sure about the party—"

"She didn't say nothing to me about it."

"I mean, the skating. Maybe it makes her skittish."

"Skittish?" He looked at me quizzically.

"Nervous," I said.

"Oh. Yeah. Well, she's nervous about everything. If I take the stairs instead of the elevator at the hospital—they might be slippery. If I walk home after dark—I might get jumped, you know. If I floss my teeth," he added, then laughed at his own joke. I was glad to see his old smile.

I stood to go. "How about if I pick you up on the twentieth, okay? The other kids would be glad to see you there."

"Okay, Miss Rainey," Martin said. "Thanks for coming by and all." He picked up Kiki and waved her minute paw at me. "Maybe I'll take Kiki down to the hospital to see James. Maybe he'd like that," he said.

"Yeah, I think he would," I said. As I said it, I believed it. I believed for the first time that maybe Angela had reason to hope. Hope was a funny thing, I thought. When you had none, gravity anchored you to the earth like lead. When hope crept in through some small crevice, it was as if you might actually fly. It was possible, anything was still possible. A boy believing his damaged brother was better off dead could, with a little hope, carry a tiny kitten inside his jacket to the brother's bedside, press the padded paws against the thin, motionless arm, and whisper, "Hang in there, buddy. I'm right here." Walking to my car, thinking about Martin, I was faintly buoyant myself.

In May, I told Lydia I thought it was time I moved out. In fact, I already had all of my things packed, two bags' worth, set beside the door. Lydia had just come home from a week-long yoga retreat that was a birthday gift from her sister, and she was energetically, yet calmly, gliding around the rooms of her apartment, checking potted plants, leafing through mail, hugging me as if we'd been separated for months. The truth was, I had relished the time alone, watching Lydia's television, buying myself groceries, and eating them without the pressure of conversation for a change. For so long I had dreaded and avoided solitude, afraid to confront the silence, especially in the dark, the space where Dill wasn't being filled by someone, anyone, else. So being alone was a revelation. I stood in it and breathed and survived.

Lydia had just been demonstrating *Tadasana,* standing firmly planted in the middle of the living room, palms open at her sides, head steady, eyes closed, breathing in and out with deliberation. "See, you just feel yourself part of the earth, attached, like a mountain, you know?" She opened her eyes and beamed at me. "Plus all the other stuff, the stretches, the saunas, the papaya smoothies for breakfast. It was like I died and went to heaven." She smiled guiltily. "I wish you could have come, Anna. It would have been so good for you to get away from everything for a while. Maybe we can set something up."

"Thanks, Lyd. I think actually I need to be here for a while. I mean, here, at work and everything—but not here, in your house. I need to move on." For the first time she noticed the luggage at the door.

"Where are you going? When did you decide this?" She seemed offended, as if we had a shared lease agreement, as if she would have to scramble to fill the vacant cat bed. "Are you going—home?" She said this so gingerly, she almost cringed, knowing as she did how I felt about the place I had shared with Dill and then abandoned. I still had not gone back, not even once. A neighbor boy I'd hired had been keeping the driveway shoveled, and then the lawn mowed and weeded, so at least outwardly it did not appear neglected. But it was possible that the rooms inside were strung with spiderwebs, the cupboards gnawed through by mice. I wasn't about to find out.

"No," I said. "I found a room on campus. The college has emptied out for the summer and then Upward Bound kids will move in for seminars and special events, and I thought it would be nice to be nearby."

"You're moving to campus. To a dorm," Lydia said, as if I had admitted I was entering a convent.

"Yes. I really want to do this. For now. For the summer. It will be kind of nice," I added lamely. I didn't know how to tell her what moved me when I moved on. Each time something small just shifted inside me and I felt tugged or nudged in some other direction. I didn't think it that radical, but I hadn't thought of how Lydia might receive the news.

"It's me, isn't it," she said finally. She was no longer standing grandly joined to the earth; her shoulders sagged, and she was running her toe along the grooves of the wooden floor. "I drive you crazy, don't I? Always analyzing, always poking and prodding. No wonder you just want to be alone." She swallowed hard.

"No!" I said. "It isn't that at all, I swear. I love being with you, you've been the best friend anyone could ask for." Better than Lexi? I heard her thinking. Perhaps Lydia's clairvoyance was contagious. "Better than anyone, even Philip or Lexi. I mean it. But don't tell them." I smiled, and she laughed.

"I've just gotten so used to having you around," she said then, coming to wrap her arms around me. I let her. I held her, too, swaying there for a long, amiable moment. Then I pulled away.

"Thank you for everything, Lydia. I don't know how to tell you how much you've helped me."

"Really?" Her eyes were watery, the fake lashes wet little brushes against her skin. I nodded, turning away to contain my own emotion. I had to go. It was time; I felt it as surely as if there were a giant clock ticking, steam rolling from underneath a train engine.

"I'll call you when I get settled," I promised, then hoisted my bags and walked out before Lydia could prolong the farewell. After all, I was merely going across town again. Bouncing from house to house like ports on a miniature voyage.

The room really was like a convent, spare, monastic, stripped bare except for a mattress and desk, a lone chair, and a built-in wardrobe with three metal hangers dangling like chimes. The walls were an ethereally pale blue, the color of nothing, and the windows opened onto a neglected tennis court, grass erupting along fault lines. I set my bags down on the bed and opened the window. The air smelled not of earth and mown lawn, as I expected, but pungent with tar. A truck rolled slowly down the street, two soiled men shoveling tar behind them as a steamroller followed like a slow, obedient pet, pressing down the black mounds till they gleamed smooth as licorice. It was mesmerizing watching them, and I did so for nearly twenty minutes. Then I turned to the small task of unpacking and settling in. I realized I had brought no bedding with me, as I had not needed any till now. I decided I would go shopping. It might be fun, like a college student, outfitting my new room.

I locked the door behind me and wandered down the long corridor. All the other rooms were open, windows ajar, being aired out for the season. It was a bit like being the only customer in a hotel, except without the front desk, or room service, or really any service at all. I knew the Upward Bound students would not be arriving for several weeks, and so I was completely alone in the entire dorm. I was not afraid, but I felt a little displaced. Where else would I go, though? I couldn't continue relying on the hospitality of friends; and I needed to stop being tended to, waited on. Here, there would be no one at the bathroom door asking, "Do you need a towel, anything?" No one standing at the refrigerator offering breakfast choices. "We have juice, bagels—no, sorry, only English muffins, and cereal. Do you want fruit with it?" Of course, I appreciated it. And at the beginning, I couldn't have functioned without it, without them. Wandering through my private dorm, I suddenly thought, This is going to be a good thing.

At the department store, I browsed the linens, finding nothing to my liking, and also thinking, These would have to be laundered before I could sleep on them, the crisp sheets folded tightly into clear vinyl bags, the chemicals wafting from blankets. Instead, I drifted to the camping supplies aisle and found an array of sleeping bags. They ranged from regular camper (flannel-lined, poly-filled) to expedition (nylon-lined, down-filled) to Arctic ("wicking" taffeta-lined, down-filled). The last was so thick that on its side it resembled a hay roll in a field, and I thought of the first person to line a sleeping bag with taffeta—had she remembered coming home from her senior prom and falling asleep in her gown, waking to discover the soothing satiny sensation against her skin? Or perhaps it was a man, reminiscing about the girl whose dress shimmered in the gymnasium light, and how he felt when his chin grazed the fabric as he danced. Years later, sitting in his office cubicle designing outdoor gear, he had a flashback and an inspiration. As I combed the aisle, I noticed that each style came in deep, moody colors of plum and forest and brick. No pastels here, though I did come across a single child-size Barbie sleeping bag, bubble-gum pink and lined with smiling flannel doll faces. I decided that, with summer approaching, the original camper bag would suit me fine. I tucked it under my arm, along with a standard-size pillow, and then, on impulse, also picked up a red lantern with a wire handle.

Back in the dorm, I unrolled my new bedding, unzipped it partway, and nestled the pillow at the top. Then I lay down to try it out.

Immediately I slid into a groove in the center of the bed, worn there by countless girls before me. I thought of them lying awake at night, lonely, wondering if they would ever fall in love. How many took boys to bed with them, careful of making noise, senses attuned like antennae to the treads of head residents? I remembered doing that as a student. Sophomore year I was dating a senior named Skip, and when I could forget his name for a few minutes, I could fall into a wordless state of bliss. In the dark dorm room, curled beside me in the small bed, he would waste no time groping through my clothing, until I pushed him away. Then he would sit up in exasperation, look at his watch, and mutter that he might as well go study. Immediately, in the harsh light, he would become a Skip once more, and I would be glad to see him go. We lasted only two months because he hated the suspense—and I loved it. I wanted to be touched and to explore, but I wasn't interested in pursuing a love affair with Skip.

Later there were other, more satisfying boyfriends, but none compared with the last; Dill was in a class by himself, in every way. I suppose one could argue that his name was as comical as Skip's, and friends did make the predictable jokes. But Dill was the only one who took the time to notice me, who loved me as no other had. Dill would say, "You are the best thing that ever happened to me," and I would fill with joy sweet as syrup being injected into my veins, and we would just lie there, wound together, content.

Lying atop my new sleeping bag, I felt stunned again that I was *here,* and he was not. Don't think about it, I warned myself. Better just to go on with the next thing.

And the next thing happened to be that I grew ravenously hungry— then realized I had no food, or any means for preparing it. What had I been thinking? Why hadn't I just rented a furnished apartment? All of a sudden the adventure paled and all I could think was how complicated the simple life was becoming. Now I would have to eat all my meals out, or find a little refrigerator. I would need a plate, a bowl, utensils, a coffeemaker. . . . It was exhausting. One thing at a time, I reminded myself. And then I remembered that it was Tuesday, the night of my weekly SOLO session—it was my fourth one, and I was getting used to the atmosphere, the others and their stories, the shouldering of sorrow, the ready advice, the knowing nods. And there was always food. I rose from my bed and headed out the door again, with a simple mission.

J oanne apologized for the "slim pickings." I stood forlornly over the table full of cheese and crackers, an ice chest packed with soft drinks. It wasn't as though she usually prepared pot roasts or fried chicken, but often there were muffins and small sandwiches; sometimes the session went on for a few hours and people needed replenishing. I layered crackers onto a paper plate and tried not to devour them in front of her. I wondered if there was time to run out for a fast-food burger, but the room suddenly began to fill with people, so I took my plate with me and sat down.

Jon Gordon, Jr., sat beside me and smiled. We had not spoken before, and I could sense that he was feeling shy. I didn't blame him. It was strange talking during breaks or after a session; once you opened up in front of a group of virtual strangers, there was little room for small talk, chitchat in the hallway. Usually what someone said when she came up to you was, "No one ever put it into words like that before, but that's *exactly how I felt.*" Or sometimes she simply put her arms around you and rocked you like a baby. At first this alarmed me. I could take it from Lexi or Lydia, but when Georgia, one of the older women, embraced me, clouded in perfume, I wanted to yank free.

Stop, I thought. You don't even know me. But she did know me, at least a little, and better than some of my close friends did. I told the group things I had never voiced before. Like the rage.

Jon Gordon, Jr., cleared his throat and said, "I should've eaten first. I had to run Celie over to soccer practice and then a friend's house and we were going to grab pizza in between, but she got invited to stay there for dinner. Then I sort of forgot about myself, and now I'm starving." He looked a little sheepish.

"I know," I said. "Me, too. And I hate to tell you, but this is all there is." I brushed crumbs from my blouse and lap and smiled back, hoping that Cheddar was not wedged between my teeth.

"You want to go have a bite somewhere, after?" he asked.

"Sure," I said. But I wasn't sure at all. While Joanne gathered everyone around and began the session, I couldn't concentrate on her words. All I could think was, Is this a date? Did he just ask me out? Dating had not once crossed my mind. My husband was gone, yes; I had come to accept that it was horribly true. But I had never entertained the notion of looking to replace him. Replace him! I felt myself go pale, my underarms dampen. It was as if Dill were in the room, watching me, daring me to think it, to think of another. *I'm not!* I silently argued.

Once, around our fifth anniversary, I was in a bookstore browsing after work. I had recently broken the pinkie finger of my left hand when it caught on a railing, and it was taped to my ring finger, obscuring the gold band and the tiny diamond. A young man seemed to shadow me through the aisles, discreetly picking up books but obviously not reading them. When I caught him staring at me, he looked quickly away, but the second time, he smiled. I smiled back. He asked me what I was reading, and I held up the book and said, "Flannery O'Connor. Have you ever read her?"

He shook his curly head. "No, but I probably should have, right?"

I laughed. I turned back to the stacks of books and pretended to choose another. I hadn't flirted in so long, it was like flexing a stiff muscle. I was tongue-tied. Then I thought, I'm happily married, there's nothing wrong with harmless conversation in a store. I decided to try to see if I still knew how to attract a man.

"This one is great," I said. "If you're looking for advice." I handed him a collection of stories by an author I hadn't even heard of.

He looked down at the cover, then at me. His eyes were brown with girlish lashes. He was very pretty. He was probably used to talking to women wherever he went. Perhaps he relied on them for advice at every turn—What should I read? What should I order? Do I look good in blue? Some men were like that, I knew, needing affirmation, needing petting.

"So, are you a bookworm?" he asked, smiling.

I tilted my head slightly as if considering. My hair fell around my jawline. "Not really," I said. "I just like the smell of books. I like bookstores, so I come to wander around, see what I find."

He grinned. I could sense him shifting toward me, his weight, his interest. Soon he would be asking my name, my phone number. "How did you hurt yourself?" he asked, indicating my finger. He touched my hand lightly, just below the bandage.

"Oh, that," I said, thinking up a good lie. "I broke up a fight in a bar." He looked skeptical, then impressed. I could feel him moving closer, I knew in a moment he would find an excuse to touch me again. "Well, I have to go," I said abruptly, tucking the books back on the shelves.

"Wait—" he said. I kept walking, not looking back. It was thrilling, knowing I could do it, and then stop when I wanted to. It might have been cruel, too, intentionally wasting his time. But I knew he would simply walk around, chagrined, until another girl walked in, and he would start all over again—a clean slate, nothing to lose, everything to gain.

When I got home, I casually told Dill about the encounter, as if it were a social experiment, though the retelling felt like a confession.

"Tell me how you did it," he said, bemused. "Did you toss your hair? Did you do that thing with your eyes?"

"What thing?"

"You know, like this—" He demonstrated as I laughed. "All wide and blinky."

"I don't do that!" I protested. Then asked coyly, "So, you aren't jealous?"

"No. Should I be?"

"Of course not. It was a stupid game."

Later, in bed, he brought it up again, and I knew then that he hadn't been completely honest. It did bother him, if only a little. He hinted, and I understood that he needed to know I was just kidding around in the bookstore. I assured him that he was the only man for me. He kissed me and fell happily asleep. I lay there awhile thinking how lucky I was, that I would never have to go out there in the world and do that for real. I had the one I wanted right here.

By the time Joanne called my name, I was so lost in thought, I heard my own voice as from some great distance murmur, "Not tonight. I mean, I don't—I can't—" I stammered and swallowed.

"It's okay," Joanne said gently, "we all have off days. You can just sit back and listen. We're here for you even in the silence, you know." And then there was silence, leaden, as I felt the others gazing at me sympathetically, Jon Gordon beside me looking and then looking away. He knew that I was answering him, not Joanne, when I spoke. You learned to develop keen perception in rooms like this. Body language, the space between words. You understood more than was said because you were so used to saying one thing in your own head and another out loud; everyone did it.

Afterward there was an awkward shuffling from chairs as Jon stood up and wrapped himself in his coat, nodded to me. "Maybe some other time," he managed to murmur.

"Okay," I said. "I mean, that would be fine. That would be nice, I think." I didn't know what else to say, and I knew I had wounded his pride, though he had to understand. He was widowed, too—surely he wasn't *looking* yet. When I turned he was gone.

All of the women except the Birkenstocks girl, Polly, were clustered together, talking intimately, and they paused to wave to me. "Bye, Anna!" they said, cheerily, kindly. "See you next week." I nodded and waved back but walked quickly out the door.

I won't be coming back, I thought. And as soon as I thought it, I knew it was true. I didn't need to keep coming here, rehashing the sorrow. It was over. Done. I was done with it. I was done with him. In my car, I sat bowed over the wheel as if in prayer, but I wasn't praying.

"You're the one who left!" I screamed in my head. "It's *over*." And then I started the engine and drove away fast, as if leaving my dead, bewildered husband standing in the parking lot watching me go.

The first night was terrible. Even the first nights with each of my friends had been fraught with anxiety, the oppression of making myself "at home" in a strange place, and then the darkness settling over me anew. I closed my eyes each time and prayed, but the words always got stuck on my tongue, like a foreign language, and I ended up whispering simply, *Please,* not knowing even what I was asking for.

In the dorm room, the dark was a heavy layer of coats. When I was young, like most children, I would play in the room with all the coats and purses of guests during my parents' rare parties. There would be a mound three feet high of wool and tartan-lined trenches, the lone mink or rabbit. I tried them all on, the women's coats (and once a man's bowler, belonging to a colleague of my father whom everyone accepted as "eccentric"), and liked to tuck my chin into the furry collars, drape myself in filmy scarves. These I carefully tucked back into coat sleeves and made sure I never gave away my rummaging tendencies. I never took anything, and I never looked into the latched handbags. One night, when a guest left early and startled me by opening the door, I had just enough time, in the dark, to dive under the pile of coats on the bed—why I didn't simply crawl under the bed, I don't know—and lie there, holding my breath, while the person sifted downward, searching. Then a hand found my leg and hesitated there. The hand, a man's I knew, from its size and pressure, traveled the rest of the way up my body, patting it, as if I were a garment with pockets and he were simply searching for the bulk of a wallet or keys. Finally, he stopped, laughed into the darkness, jerked a coat free from the pile, and left the room. I lay there for a few minutes more, suffocating beneath the weight of fabric, and then I slid out, breathing hard. I never did it again.

Afterward, I began to associate darkness with a kind of weight, pressing down, engulfing the room and everything in it, including me, along with a kind of dread of being grabbed, even though I knew I hadn't really been in danger. It was just the anticipation that scared me. Early in our marriage, I admitted this to Dill, and he laughed, pulled me close. "Do you want me to get a night-light?" he asked.

"Don't mock me," I said, and he didn't. And I noticed that after that he always left a light on in the bathroom, or closet, so that, as I fell asleep, I could watch the stripe of light.

Cocooned in my sleeping bag, with a street lamp burned out and no lights anywhere in the building, I felt the old dread well up, and now there was no one at all in the next room. Then I remembered the lantern I'd bought earlier that day. I reached out and switched it on. A soft, cheery ring of light burst against the wall, and instantly the room changed a little. The lantern flickered like Tinker Bell, hovering just close enough to say, "Hey, it's okay. I'll stay here while you sleep, I'll keep watch." And it worked. I slept.

A t the bank on my lunch hour, I waited in line behind the velvet ropes and stanchions, though only one other customer was ahead of me. When he turned from the teller's window to go, he spotted me in a glance and then stopped in his tracks, grinning.

"Anna? Anna Rainey?" he said, coming toward me.

"Yes?" I said, as if I weren't really sure myself.

"I'm Ian Patterson, one of Dill's clients! He worked on our gallery campaign, remember? He did such a great job! I came to his office at your house a couple of times."

I remembered Ian now, enthusiastic and effusive as ever, and how Dill had once joked to me that Ian had a crush on him. Ian was chattering on about Dill, and I tried to listen, caught off guard by his jocular mood. Then I heard him saying, "So how is he?"

"Dill?" I said, bewildered.

"Yeah, I haven't seen him in ages, since I relocated to Minneapolis last year. It's been a really good move for me, but I still have some family living here, and had a savings account I never bothered to close,

I'm not sure why. Not that there was much in it, I'm terrible at saving!" He laughed, and I wondered if I should, too, but I stood there, realizing I was gripping the velvet rope in one fist. "Anyway, I have to run, I'm meeting some old friends for lunch." He glanced at his watch and smiled again. "Well, it's great to see you, Anna! Tell Dill hello for me, will you?"

My mouth opened and closed like a mute's, desperate for sound to come out, but instead I found myself nodding. After he left I wondered why I didn't tell him. Yet how could one slip those words, "He's dead," into a ceaseless flow of good cheer?

"Miss?" a voice called to me from the teller's window, and I walked automatically over to her, handed her my check, and silently signed my name.

Philip called me at work to ask how I was doing. "How's dorm life?" he said. Like everyone else, he had heard about my peculiar arrangement and hinted in an effort not to offend me. "If you ever get tired of the other girls, and the lousy food, you're welcome to come back here. Prince Charles promises to be good." What he meant, of course, was that *he* would be good.

I laughed, pretending I didn't catch the innuendo. "Thanks, but I'm fine. I'm getting used to the—solitude. And I got a fridge and a few things to keep me going. I even bought a CD player."

At night now I could sing along with Isaac Hayes or Billie Holiday and wallow in self-pity. I listened to Irish folk music, and though I had no Irish roots, Dill had, so whenever I heard the heartbreaking fiddle, I would feel I had lost not just a husband but a homeland, everything I had known from the beginning of time. I also seemed to have developed a strange literary antenna, which turned me, in libraries and bookstores, toward words of sorrow. Zippered into my cocoon, I recited quotes like counting sheep: "I hate the day, because it lendeth light/To see all things, but not my love to see" (Edmund Spenser). "He is dead and gone, lady,/He is dead and gone,/At his head a grass-green turf,/At his heels a stone" (William Shakespeare). Emily Dickinson was another favorite. I probably could have written reams of my own poetry, had I been so inclined, or remembered to purchase paper and pencils. And so on I went, day after day after day, living my life, leading my students, washing my clothing, eating my meals, and reading my morbid books. Sometimes I let myself believe that light would part the clouds, eventually, and all would return "to normal."

Of course, I didn't say any of this to Philip. When he asked if I wanted to have lunch, I said sure. We met at the local vegetarian deli called Big Sprouts and sat at a table outside, since it was nearly summer now and the sun was irresistible in Michigan, rare as it was. A red-striped umbrella covered our table, but I wore sunglasses. I smiled at my old friend like the old days. Easier this way, to pretend.

"So," I said, after we had eaten, made small talk.

"I was just going to say the same thing," Philip said. Then he leaned in and wiped a bit of mustard from my lip and said softly, "Are you really all right, Anna?" He had a deeply pitying look in his eyes.

Suddenly I grew angry, self-righteous. I said, "You know what? *Life goes on.* What else can I do? What do you want me to say? I feel like everyone thinks I'm so fragile. But I'm not made of glass." I looked down at my plate of roasted root vegetables and sweet potato chips and stirred them with a fork.

"I'm sorry," he said. "I know what it's like to be—pigeonholed. People expect you to be a certain way, and they don't know what to do when you reveal another side." I looked at him, wondering what he was getting at. "I mean," he went on, "there's more to me than comic relief, believe it or not."

I laughed, not meaning to. "Sorry," I said.

"It's okay." He shrugged, took a long sip of water. "I guess I just wanted you to know, Anna, that you don't have to see me when you're feeling fine, then run away when you're not."

"Is that what you think? That I left your place to go to Lydia's because I wasn't in a *good mood*?"

"I guess I thought you thought I couldn't handle your grief, that I could only joke and try to keep you cheerful. I mean, that is what I tried to do, cheer you up, but I wanted to do more than that—"

I felt suddenly stricken in the glaring sunshine, the cloying closeness of the other tables, though the other diners were deep in their own conversations. Someone nearby laughed, someone else muttered, "Oh, damn," and I could hear water trickling from a table to the cement.

"I was only trying to be there for you," Philip said lamely.

"I have to go," I said, and I stood up and left quickly, leaving Philip looking down at his lap, rubbing his temple with one hand.

He phoned an hour later to apologize. "I didn't mean it like that," he said.

"I know," I said.

"I wish we could go back to the way things used to be," he said.

"Me too," I said. I wanted things—*everything*—the way they used to be, but I knew it wasn't possible. Nothing endures but change, I thought. I also knew by heart one of Heraclitus's lesser-quoted proverbs: "Man, like a light in the night, is kindled and put out." Just like that, like the candle on a cake, he was gone. It occurred to me that Dill's birthday had come and gone in April and I'd never noticed it— or refused to. The last time he blew out candles and made a wish there were thirty-six. I remembered pressing them gently into the frosting one by one, laughing and teasing him that I had used up three boxes of candles. If only I'd known that would be the last time. We both would have stood there and wished and prayed with all our might. We would have made every moment count. But didn't every moment count, even if you weren't counting? Perhaps they were all the more poignant because you didn't know what was coming.

"Anna?" Philip called into my ear, and I remembered where I was.

"What?"

"I really am sorry. I wasn't trying to take advantage. I just wanted you to know how much I care about you—as a friend. And I don't want that to change."

"Okay," I said. You're no fun, I thought, and I could have been referring to both of us.

Martin came to my office the day before the end-of-the-year ceremony. "I should've called, I guess, but I was in the neighborhood just walking around and I thought you might be here." I pushed my papers away and sat up to listen. "I can't come tomorrow. There's— Something came up." He stared at the floor, rubbed one elbow, then scratched his ear.

"What is it?" I asked. I dreaded the answer, but if James had died, would Martin be here?

He shrugged. "I just can't. I don't belong here anymore. I haven't done anything—I haven't been working."

As I looked at his sorrowful face, something happened inside me, like the child suddenly turned into the mother, the adult with the answers. Not having children, I thought this must be what it's like. And if sorrow is a heavy pair of shoes, this was slipping for a few moments into sleek high heels, with delicate straps. I stood up then, and strode around my desk to put an arm around Martin's shoulder, pulled him under my wing. "Is there something I can do to help?"

"I don't know," he said. "I mean, I don't know what you could do, Miss Rainey."

"Well," I said, "for starters I could give you a ride tomorrow night, so your mom wouldn't have to leave the hospital. Okay?"

"Okay," he said finally, shuffling his giant shoes across the carpet as he left.

The next evening, when I drove to Martin's house, he was sitting on the porch again, just like the last time, except that now the kitten was mitt-size, prowling around behind Martin.

"Ready?" I asked.

He stood up. "I still feel stupid, you know, going to this like I deserve it."

"Let me decide what you deserve right now—you're being way too hard on yourself." I bent to pet Kiki. "She's really grown."

"Yeah, now she's a handful," Martin said, scowling a little at the cat. "Every day it's something new—dead mouse, dead bird, or parts of a dead bird. It's disgusting."

"Well, it's what cats do, a friend once told me."

"I know, but maybe they should've evolved past that now, with Kitten Chow and all that expensive stuff."

I laughed at this logic. As I started to lead Martin to my car, I noticed he was holding back. I thought for a moment he wasn't coming after all, and I prepared to reiterate my encouragement—or berate him—but he'd simply paused to talk to a neighbor over the low hedgerow. The young man next door was waving a garden hose gently back and forth over a droopy line of petunias. His head was down as if he couldn't look Martin in the eyes. Now and then he would glance up, smile sadly, and then turn back to the watering. I realized then who he was.

"I want you to meet someone," Martin called to me. I walked back. "This is Jay Hernandez," he said, and the man nodded slightly. "Jay, this is Miss Rainey, my favorite teacher." I smiled at that, not bothering to correct him; "academic adviser" sounded a little lofty anyway.

"Nice to meet you," I said.

"You, too," he said. There was an embarrassed pause, and I filled it by telling Martin that we might be late.

Martin said, "Well, we gotta go. Jay, you take care, okay?" He patted Jay on the back, then strode to my car and got in the passenger side.

Before I followed, I couldn't help turning to look at Jay. He was beautiful, young, but with the older face of someone who has lived a long life in a short time. His eyes were dark and soft, though sorrowful, and he was tall and lean, probably once bulkier but stripped of weight by anxiety and guilt. I knew the guilt part. Even if he blamed the ice, the brakes locking, the wheels spinning out of his control, a part of him would always think, *If only.*

In my car, Martin said, "He's a mess." I didn't say anything, concentrated on where I had to turn. Martin rolled the window down and leaned an elbow out. "You know, he can't forgive himself."

"You mean, because of the accident," I said.

"Yeah. But it was an *accident,*" he said firmly, in a tone that made me think he had been practicing the sentence. Perhaps his mother had forced him to repeat it, hand on a Bible. "Forgive us our trespasses as we forgive those who trespass against us."

"It's hard to be the one responsible," I said. "You don't get over that very easily."

"But we don't blame him, my mom and me," Martin said.

"It doesn't matter," I said. It seemed so obvious, I wondered why I had to explain. Suddenly I didn't want to try, so I turned on the radio and hummed along.

"You know, he won't drive, now," Martin went on. "Not at all. He walks everywhere."

"Nothing wrong with that," I said. And then we were at the parking lot, so I didn't have to say any more.

The kids lined up like shiny pennies, clean and scrubbed, noses gleaming under the bright lights. Some of the girls wore high-heeled sandals to reveal carefully painted toenails. Hair was combed, lips glossed, eyes sparkling. Only half of the boys wore ties, but the others at least had bothered to tuck in shirttails, wear pants with belts. Every year, the same energy buzzed through the room, the expectation and pride at an all-time high. We were gathered in one of the auditoriums on campus, to accommodate students and their parents. There were eighteen graduates, all of them accepted at colleges or universities for the fall. The others were there for support—and to receive their own awards. We made a point of acknowledging accomplishments, not as tokens but as incentives; kids love to hold small trophies or certificates with their names in inky calligraphy. Some of the seniors would receive scholarships, others paid summer internships; we worked the entire city system to get funding and professional connections. And it paid off. Now here they were, all of them, including Martin. He had taken a seat in a back row but was as bright-eyed as the others. I saw some of them reaching over to slap him, welcoming him back.

There was great applause when I introduced the valedictorian, Amber Gonzales. She stood up on her spindly stockinged legs in heels and strode to the stage, took her place at the podium. She was, in fact, not first but twenty-first in her senior class at the high school, but as far as we were concerned, she was number one. The others had chosen her unanimously, and now she stood, smiling crookedly at her peers and friends, her written speech trembling a little in her slender hands. I sat to the side, watching her, watching the beaming crowd who waited with anticipation as if it were the Oscars.

"My name is Amber Antonia Herrera Gonzales," she said, her voice high and thin in the microphone, "and I am going to the University of Michigan." The applause drowned out her next sentence. The rest of her speech, delivered grinning, exhorted the younger students never to give up, or "slack off, or be lazy" but to persevere, because "nobody's gonna do it for you."

When the cheering tapered off a little, Jillian stood up to present the awards, gold-glazed trophies and Upward Bound diplomas for each of the graduates, and then Jeremy handed out certificates of merit to the younger students. Afterward, we all gathered around long tables of cake and rose-colored punch. Some kids jokingly offered each other toasts with their plastic cups, others devoured the cake, returning for seconds. Two of the senior girls asked to have a photo taken with me and I obliged. Others came up to introduce me to their parents and shyly thank me. I nodded, smiled, and wished them well. The room was filled to the brim with words, everyone talking at once, a constant, happy hum.

When I finally went home, slipped off my shoes, and lay down on my padded sleeping bag, I thought, There they go. All of those wise, confident kids, throwing themselves out into the world. And I envied them with all my heart, so new and unscathed. And then, with my trenchant streak of gloom, I also thought, They have no idea what might hit them, pull their legs out from under them.

T hey've lost their heads," my mother said over the phone.

"Who?" It was Saturday morning and I was barely awake.

"The gnomes. They're headless, every single one of them. Can you believe someone would do that?"

"What are you talking about?"

"Vandals," she said, sighing out of impatience with me or disgust over society, or both. "Kids, I suppose, but who knows. All I know is they are lying all over the yard, all eight of them, and their heads are gone, cracked right off and tossed aside. Who would do such a thing?"

"I don't know," I said, sitting up in bed and squinting at the clock. It read 6:45. "Mom, do you know what time it is? What are you doing up this early?"

Her voice wavered. "I didn't know who to call. The police wouldn't do anything, I'm sure. They would just think I was some dotty old woman."

I sighed. "How about if I come over a little later, after I'm more awake?"

"That would be nice, honey. I'd really appreciate it. I'll make coffee. And I have cinnamon buns from Hefner's bakery, the good ones, so don't eat first, okay?"

I fell back asleep for about an hour, then resigned myself to rising and tending to my mother. I hadn't seen her in a few weeks and felt guilty about it. Yet the thought of sitting at her table and peering out at all those queer stone figures disturbed me, and my disturbance was exacerbated by my mother's even queerer attachment to them. Maybe she had some obscure Medusan disorder which turned hapless visitors into stone. I knew it was simply fatigue that piqued my imagination, and I dressed, needing the coffee and sugar my mother had offered. Needing, also, to see her and assure myself that she wasn't crazy.

Before she retired—claiming arthritis, but I suspected it was really grief—my mother used to tailor dresses and trousers for regular customers, who dropped their clothes off at her back door. My mother would need only one quick fitting to pin hemlines or pinch in side seams. She was nimble and precise, and when I was a child she always had fabric laying across her lap in the evenings. My father called her Queen Seamstress, and lavished praise on her work. Perhaps that was why she had come somewhat unhinged after his death. There was no one to affirm her, to let her know that she mattered. I certainly didn't help much.

When I arrived, she was in the yard, surveying the destruction. Sure enough, eight gnomes lay decapitated on the grass, surrounded by scattered shards of cement, brightly colored bits of caps, and one white swirl of beard, like a fossilized ice cream cone.

"It's terrible," I said, bending down to brush dust from the chest of one. My mother turned, and I saw that she was weeping. "Oh, Mom," I said. "Don't worry, I'll help you clean this up, and we can go get some more if you want. Maybe you could install a spotlight in the yard—" I was grasping for inspiration, something to calm and reassure her. But she was shaking her head.

"Oh, it's not that," she said, wiping her eyes with one finger under each lens of her glasses. "I don't care about replacing them. I mean, they were adorable, but it's just that— I don't know. I just don't understand why people can't just let other people *be*. Why should it bother someone that I like to decorate my yard, make the world a little more cheerful? Is there something wrong with that?"

"No, there isn't," I said. And I understood then what had motivated her to work so hard at populating her backyard. There was nothing pathological or even particularly eccentric about it; they cheered her up. When she rose each morning, she probably smiled, seeing the tiny characters frozen in jaunty poses, or serenely holding a bouquet of flowers, like the fairy in the corner of the yard, festooned with stone daisies. I felt ashamed that I had derided her, lamented to Lydia that my mother was insane. She was just lonely. I stepped across the debris and put my arms around her. We had never been close physically, and it felt strange at first, holding my own mother, feeling the ribbing of her thin cardigan against my chin. She sniffled a little, then pulled away.

"Well," she said. "What's done is done, right? Let's have something to eat, we can clean this up later."

We went inside and sat together, leisurely stirring our coffee, breaking off syrupy strips of cinnamon buns and murmuring our pleasure. And for once, I sat still, in no hurry to run off. I looked out at the remaining stone children, sun gleaming on their painted smiles, and felt time standing perfectly still.

Joanne called, cheerfully anxious. Apparently she'd left several messages on Lydia's machine, though Lydia was out of town for a former boyfriend's opening at a gallery in New York. When she returned, Lydia phoned and breathlessly told me all about the show, but more about the former—now current—boyfriend, Willie. After twenty minutes of blissful details, including some sexual that I preferred not to know about, Lydia suddenly exclaimed, "Oh, and Joanne Someone called here about five times wondering if you were all right. I was here the last time and so I just gave her your new number. I hope you don't mind. I didn't tell her it was a dorm room."

I laughed and told Lydia I wasn't ashamed of my living situation. "I like it here, it's very quiet and simple."

"That's good, I suppose, but we should go out sometime, you know, catch up and get a little drunk. It would be good for you."

"Okay," I said.

"Hey," Lydia said. "I just remembered who Joanne is—she's from your group, right? Are you still going? Is it helping?"

"Yes, no, and not really," I answered. "I mean, it wasn't bad at first. Probably it was even a little cathartic. But after a while I decided I didn't need to keep going; it was getting repetitive, you know?"

"Mm," Lydia said, and I didn't know if she was listening or sorting through her mail and tuning out. But then she said, "Well, I'm glad you gave it a try, anyway. But I wouldn't give up so fast, Anna. Things like this don't go away overnight. It takes months, maybe years. Just be patient." I thought, What does she know?

"Well, support groups aren't for everyone," I said, then lied and told her I had to go because I had a meeting. As soon as I hung up, the phone rang again and it was Joanne.

"Your ears must have been burning," I said. "I was just talking about you with my friend Lydia. She gave me your messages."

"Good. Listen, Anna, I have been worried about you, and so have the others." I cringed at the sound of it—the others, as if I'd escaped from a cult. I pictured them, perfumy Georgia and the other women, and Polly in her Birkenstocks, all of them chanting with their arms outstretched toward me. I didn't, however, picture Jon Gordon, Jr., there. I imagined him sitting at home with his mournful daughter,

Celie, hunched over homework, wiping away tears. It broke my heart.

"I just needed—a break," I said to Joanne. I sat down on my bed and scratched my bare leg. It was ten o'clock and I was in pajamas, ready to lie down and read. "It's nothing personal," I added. "Sometimes it just doesn't seem like the right thing, you know, to tell other people what you think and feel all the time. It just wasn't the right time for me."

"A time to keep silence and a time to speak," Joanne said with a slightly lofty intonation. "Ecclesiastes three, verse seven. I tell people that all the time. And you know, you can still come to the meetings and not speak, if you'd like. It's perfectly acceptable."

"I know that," I said, trying not to sound impatient.

"Well, I just wanted you to know you have friends out here."

"Thank you," I said, and hung up.

I thought about that, friends out there, and wondered if maybe she was right. I remembered how I'd felt when Vera spoke up that first night, how sharp my connection to her had been. And how tender I'd felt toward the others, including Jon, even after his fumbling offer of dinner. Maybe I hadn't been fair to him. I hoped he wasn't wounded by my absence. Then I thought, I'm sure he has other things on his mind. And again I pictured his daughter lying alone in her bed, just like me, only motherless, which I supposed was a shade much darker than widowed.

During a downpour, I was driving home from 7-Eleven, where I had stocked up on the evening's junk food, a bag full of candy bars and chips. A cherry Slurpee was balanced between my thighs, numbing them. When I stopped at a red light, I glanced to the side and saw a man waiting on the sidewalk, head bowed underneath a sweatshirt hood, which provided little relief from the rain. He was so soaking wet I pitied him, thinking I should do something, though I knew better than to pick up strange men in my car. However, I'd had only one experience with a hitchhiker, and it had been strangely uplifting.

When I was ten, my parents and I were driving from Michigan to Minnesota to visit my aunt and uncle, and my only three cousins. I spent most of the trip staring out of the window of the backseat or drawing on my Etch-A-Sketch and eating animal crackers, though I thought I was too old for them. Still, I carefully chose from the box, favoring the lions. I liked to nibble their curled manes from their heads till they looked more like monkeys. My parents, as usual, talked together up front. At some point in the journey, they began arguing, which was unusual, and I perked up to hear why. Apparently, we had passed a hitchhiker a mile or so back, and my mother thought we ought to be Good Samaritans and offer a ride, while my father said it was, "foolhardy."

"He looked pitiful," my mother said.

"He could be drunk, or stoned, or on the lam. All of which, I suppose, are pitiable conditions."

I asked what a lam was and was ignored. They debated some more. Finally my father pulled to the side of the road and turned to my mother. "You really want to pick up a total stranger and let him into our family car?"

My mother considered. "Yes," she said. "It's the Christian thing to do."

It was strange, my parents arguing heatedly, my mother suddenly religious. We attended church, the three of us, though my mother seemed to go for the socializing after the service, my father for a nap during, and I went along having no choice, of course. But outside of church, beyond the realm of sleepy sacred Sundays, I rarely heard my parents discussing their feelings on faith. Every now and then we said grace at the dinner table, and my mother reminded me to say my prayers as she turned off my light, offering no suggestion as to how that might be done. As with most things, my mother assumed I understood how to pray. Usually I lay in the sudden darkness and whispered, "Now I lay me down to sleep," having heard it somewhere. It was a comforting refrain. I never learned the rest of the rhyme, so I followed up with a short litany of requests that changed slightly over time. First it was for a sister, then a dog or cat, settling on a bike with hand brakes, which I did receive, a kind of answer to prayer, I supposed.

In the front seat, my father sighed and relented. He craned his neck so that he could look through the rear window, right arm slung over the seat back, and to my amazement, put the car in reverse. There was no traffic whatsoever, so he drove a mile and a half backward, until the pitiable figure reappeared, growing larger. My father stopped the car beside him.

"So, you need a ride?" he asked, rather jovially considering his earlier mood. The man nodded, tentative. "All right then, get in. But we are only going as far as the next town, twenty miles, for gas."

"That's fine by me," the man said, getting in the backseat beside me. My father put the car back in drive, saying nothing more, while my mother gave a small, satisfied smile. However, she also seemed a little taken aback, given the man's filthy condition, which wasn't quite so apparent from a distance. After she asked him where he was headed, and he said, "California, ultimately," she smiled and turned back around, also silent.

The hitchhiker, possibly a menace to society, was sitting less than an arm's width from me. I could smell his body odor, like the hot gymnasium at school after the older boys ran around yelling and throwing balls. And I could see, close-up, the terrible condition of his blue jeans, which looked as if they had been gathering dirt for weeks or months, or longer. I swooned. I leaned a little closer to my window and, trying not to appear rude, rolled it slowly down a few more inches. At that moment, the passenger seemed to take notice of me for the first time.

"Hi," he said. He smiled, and the skin around his eyes crinkled with dirt.

"Hi," I said.

"What are you, about fourth grade?"

"Fifth."

"Oh." He didn't ask my name or anything else, as if that were all he could think of. I thought of other adults I'd encountered, and how my name, age, and rank in school were about all any of them could muster, so it wasn't that unusual. I thought then about all the things inside me that no one knew about. My head full of knowledge and ideas and imaginings that were all my own. It filled me with a sudden euphoria, a strange rush of self-love and power. It was as if, sitting there with a man dropped in from who-knew-where, encased in his own drama and experiences and memories, I understood all at once what it meant to be wholly, singularly, secretly me. I was so thrilled and almost religiously grateful that when we finally stopped at a Shell to fill up, and the man got out, thanking us for the ride, I beamed, wanting somehow to thank *him.*

Idling at the intersection in the pouring rain, remembering the hitchhiker, I suddenly recognized the face that upturned briefly to check the traffic light. It was Jay. I beeped my horn and waved. He looked, squinting, not recognizing me. I rolled down the window and called out, "Hi! It's me, Anna, Martin's—teacher."

"Oh!" he called back, smiling. "How're you doing?"

"Do you want a ride?" I yelled back, because the light had turned green and cars behind me were honking their irritation. "Come on."

He ran across the street, through a sea of puddles, and opened the passenger door. As soon as he was in, I accelerated. "I don't know how you can be out in this," I said.

"It came on kind of sudden," he said, looking embarrassed as he wiped water from his face with his hands. His clothes were drenched; tiny rivulets pooled in the seat. "Sorry," he said, looking down at it.

"It's not a new car," I said, laughing. "It was ten years old when we bought it." There it was, that *we.* It was the first time I had said it out loud to anyone. Before Jay could notice or ask, I said, "There are some napkins in the glove box if you want to dry your face."

"That's okay," he said, so polite. We said nothing more for a few more minutes until I realized I was driving automatically toward his house. "Were you going home?" I asked then. "I just assumed— But I can drive you wherever you need to go."

"Thanks. Home is good," he said, staring at the dashboard and then through the windshield, shifting in his seat and tugging on the seat belt like someone who had never been inside a car before. It occurred to me that his choice not to drive may have included riding, too; perhaps I had pushed him to do something he wasn't ready to do. He seemed grateful, though, thanking me for the ride before we had even arrived at his house. When I pulled to the curb, Jay opened his door and started to get out.

"How are you doing?" I heard myself asking.

Jay looked at me. The belated timing must have seemed odd. "Um, fine," he said, pausing with the door half open, one leg outside in the rain, unsure whether to pull it back in or get out. He smiled awkwardly.

"No, I mean, really—how are you?"

He knew then what I meant, and he looked away. I thought, It's none of my business, I shouldn't have spoken, but he looked back, into my eyes, and I saw that his were watery. "Not so great. But thank you for asking."

"Would you like to have coffee sometime?" I blurted. It wasn't like a date, of course, I told myself; he was much too young. I could just help him, talk a little, like with Martin. We all needed a sympathetic ear. I could be his SOLO group.

"Sure. That'd be nice." Jay smiled again, but with more sincerity.

"Okay, I'll see you," I said.

"Okay," he said, practically lunging out of the car, though he turned to look back at me and wave from the walkway. As I drove away, I wondered what I thought I was getting myself into, but it had seemed like the right thing to do. And I thought, That is all we can do in this world—offer a ride to a pitiful person, reach past our own self-constructed walls and try to help.

One Sunday, the beginning of summer, Lexi invited me to the beach. Soon her house would be filled with other friends and visiting relatives, but she promised that, since it was early in the season, it would be just us. When I arrived, there were signs of life in the neighboring cottages, car trunks yawning open, piles of beach chairs just hosed clean and dripping in driveways. Overhead, a thickly green arch of leaves filtered out the sun, leaving me chilled. But as soon as I stepped out of the trees into the clearing, down the long, battered wooden stairway winding down the dune, it was like walking into another season. The sky sprung wide, the sun was blinding, the sand too hot to stand in for long.

Lexi and I followed Penny, who raced ahead, seeming not even to touch the steps as she flew down. We left our shoes at the bottom of the stairs and joined her running across the wide white beach toward the lake.

"Yikes!" yelled Penny, who was the first to plant her feet in the water. "It's freezing to death!"

We laughed and sat down on our towels. Lexi told Penny it was too soon to swim. "Wait about six weeks," she joked.

Penny frowned. "I want to swim now," she said.

"Suit yourself," Lexi said, "But you'll turn blue."

Penny looked at her mother skeptically. Then she turned back around and waded slowly in to her shins, cringing. She was wearing a sparkly purple swimsuit, with a ruffle around the neckline. She kept tugging at it as if it were too tight.

"That is the dumbest suit," Lexi told me. "I tried to talk her out of it, but you know how little girls are—they would rather look like pageant contestants than be comfortable."

"That's funny, I never did. I always wanted to wear shorts on the beach." I was wearing shorts now, over my tank suit.

"Really? You didn't have a bikini?" Lexi asked.

I laughed. "Once, when I was in high school, but it was gingham and someone called me Gidget, so I never wore it again. Plus, I always hated swimming."

Penny screeched then, turning our attention back to her; she was only yelping over the cold. Nearly waist-deep now, arms tucked up against her sides, shoulders hunched, she looked miserable, but she was grinning at us. Her hair was pulled into a tight little ponytail high on her head like a fountain. The sun glinted off the sequins of her suit, and one of her ruffled straps had slipped down.

"She really does look like a beauty queen," I said.

"Yeah," said Lexi, "Little Miss Wait-on-Me."

I laughed, but my friend went on more seriously, "You wouldn't believe how consuming it is having a kid. I mean, of course, I love her to bits, but night and day, it's all about what she needs and what she wants and if she's sick or cold, or outgrown her shoes. Last week she kept moaning about her feet, how they hurt, and I told her to quit whining. Then I happened to measure her feet at a shoe store and she had been wearing shoes nearly two sizes too small! I just didn't think! It's always something. You're lucky you don't have any kids." Then she looked at me, aghast, realizing what she had said. "Anna, I didn't mean it like that. I mean—"

"It's okay," I said, running my hands around me in the sand, creating wider and wider rings around my body. "We never talked about kids, it always seemed like there was time for that later." I paused, swallowed. "I don't know if we ever would have. Who knows?"

Lexi said nothing. Then, she said, "With kids you never have peace of mind, because something could always happen." It seemed a strange way of offering comfort, to remind me how much more I could lose, though she probably hadn't meant it that way.

"Hey, how is that little boy?" she asked me then. "The one in the coma?"

"Same," I said. "As far as they know, from scans and tests, his brain is fine, but he won't wake up."

"Gosh, that's sad."

"Yes, it is. But his mother won't give up hope."

"Mothers never do," Lexi said knowingly.

"His brother, Martin, told me it would be better if he would just die, but I told him it wouldn't. Now I'm not so sure," I said.

"Well, of course you had to tell him that. What else could you say?"

"I know. But I hate to give people false hope."

Lexi looked at me, shielding her eyes from the sun. "You don't know if it's false, though, do you? No one ever knows until the end. Until then, there's always some hope, even if it's just a shred."

I nodded, looked back over the horizon. I had been the same way, of course, until the end. Lexi seemed about to say something else, to impart some more wisdom, but then she stood and hollered, "Penny! That's far enough! Come here and warm up a little while." She sat back down and sighed as Penny obediently but slowly slogged out of the cold water. Lexi turned to me. "Boy, we really know how to have a good time on the beach, don't we!" I laughed. The morbid subject was dropped.

I looked out across the endless water, where the sky was just a shade lighter blue, the air so still around us I could hear people talking a quarter mile down the beach. A perfect day. Time crawled. We sun-burned, waded, ate peanut butter sandwiches without crusts and orange slices dripping from plastic Baggies. Penny dug tunnels in the sand, demanded her mother help her, and finally fell asleep underneath Lexi's canvas umbrella.

"I wish I could do that," Lexi noted, gently rubbing her daughter's sweaty forehead, where the bangs were painted in dark swirls. "You know, just give in to my own desires at a whim." Lexi looked at me. "Want to go swimming?" she asked, smiling.

I shook my head. "It's against my religion."

"Come on! You're from Michigan! You can handle a little arctic water." She was already walking the few yards to the shore, gingerly wading in, still grinning. "It's perfect!"

"Liar," I said. I stood up, but ventured only to the very edge, where the foam laced the sand. Lexi was in to her waist, quietly screaming. Then she dove, a shallow dolphin dive, and emerged gleaming an instant later. She waved me in, but I stood my ground.

"I'll just watch," I said. I sprawled back on the towel. Lexi dove again, thrashing gracefully about in an obvious effort to warm herself. From a distance it was difficult to tell her age, or even her gender. I remembered standing on the beach each summer watching Dill swim further and further out. He always paused and turned back to wave to me, knowing I wouldn't follow. He had long since stopped begging me to join him, to learn to swim. Once, he got me in far enough to float, his arms holding me at the surface.

"If you let go, I'll kill you," I said, squinting up at him.

"I won't, I promise," he said. "Besides, you weigh nothing."

I laughed then. It was true, I had to admit; the one good thing about the water was how free and weightless I felt, how safe swaying on his forearms. It was very sensual. But after a while I just wanted to be back on dry ground, warmed by the sun. Dill resumed swimming. Like Lexi he arced and surfaced over and over, then strode back in toward me, shaking like a dog, spraying icy droplets over me. He lay down on top of me, pressing his entire cold, wet body over my dry skin, though I warned him that other people were staring.

"Let 'em," he said. "It'll give them something to talk about, the poor sex-starved bastards."

"Dill!" I said, pushing him off. He just laughed, rolled over in the sand until he looked like breaded cutlet.

Lexi suddenly flopped beside me, startling me. "Okay," she said, smiling, invigorated. "That was fun, but insanely cold! No wonder Penny finally passed out."

Later, when Penny woke up, groggy and sandy and out of sorts, we packed up our things and trudged back up the stairs, all one hundred and twenty-two of them. At the top I stopped to catch my breath and turned to look back across the lake. If I looked hard enough, I could imagine Dill still down there, splashing and waving to me.

The maintenance staff swept through my dorm the next morning, preparing the rooms and bathrooms anew for seventy-five Upward Bound students. They would live on campus for six weeks, thirty-nine of them girls who would invade my quiet floor. Initially I had looked forward to it, imagined sitting around the common room watching television with them, braiding hair, and listening to their private lives, like an extended slumber party. Now, however, I braced myself. I liked living alone in my little room, wandering the long empty corridors, showering in any one of the ten stalls each morning. I wasn't prepared for noise, laughter, girls tapping on my door to ask advice. I wondered if I should move out, find an apartment in town, perhaps above the coffee shop, so I could wake to the heady aroma of French roast and sit at a window watching people coming and going. It sounded like too much effort. I was here, settled in. I didn't want to move.

I dried my hair beside the open window, relishing the warmth, and shook the remaining sand out of my shoes. Like a child I was still attuned to the rhythm of the school year, and it felt strange to be dressing for work on a summer day, especially after a day at the beach. I considered calling in sick, playing hooky, but I had too much to do.

On my way out I was surprised to find Jay, pacing the sidewalk in front of my dorm. He smiled shyly. "I got your address from Martin," he explained.

"How did he know I lived here?"

Jay shrugged. "I don't know." He folded his arms over his chest and seemed to be trying to find his nerve. Finally, he said, "I thought about what you said and I wondered if we could have coffee." He spoke flatly, but his eyebrows were raised in a question.

"Sure," I said automatically, not knowing what else to say; I couldn't turn him away now. "I guess I don't have to be right on time for work." In spite of my good intentions the day I'd offered him a ride, I wondered what he had inferred from my invitation. Surely he was aware of our age difference, and the fact that I was a married woman. Was.

I fell in line beside him, and we began walking the six blocks to the coffee shop. The sun was bright, slicing angles into the sidewalks and across walls. We both looked around us, as if searching for a topic to spark a conversation, but both of us remained silent. It occurred to me that Jay was like me that way, naturally shy, reluctant to reveal or unveil too much too soon. I didn't mind the silence. He tucked his hands into his pockets as if resigned.

At the door, Jay stepped aside to let me go in first, a subtle, chivalrous action that amused me, but I accepted and walked ahead. We found a booth in the back corner, and I glanced around at the familiar artwork as if seeing it for the first time. I had a hard time meeting the brown eyes across from me.

"I hope you don't mind me asking you here," he said softly. "I mean, I don't want to make you nervous or anything."

I looked at him. "You don't," I said, realizing when I met his eyes that it was true.

"I just— Well, you seem like a really nice person, and Martin says you're a good listener." I smiled at this compliment, and Jay went on. "So, I thought maybe we could talk. I mean, I know you lost someone— I'm sorry about your husband, that must be really hard. And I—I just don't know anyone else who would know what it's like to be sad. All the time."

I wondered if my sadness was so clear to others, though I tried all day to hide it. Perhaps it was like the mound of a hunchback, impossible to camouflage even with a voluminous jacket. I didn't know what to say, but I felt he needed something. So I told the truth.

"People tell you it will get better, that time heals all wounds, you know, just keep truckin' and all that. Keep your chin up." I paused. "But every day you still feel mostly the same as the day before." Jay nodded sadly.

We sat in silence for a long time, and I looked at his hands folded on the table. They were strong hands, with thick fingers but rounded, clean nails. Calluses bumped along the outer edges of his index fingers, and I wondered what he did for work, but I didn't think it the time to ask, to make small talk. Staring at his hands reminded me of something. "Martin told me James moved his hands, squeezed Martin's fingers. Isn't that a good sign?" I said. "Maybe he's doing better."

Jay shrugged, leaned heavily back against the seat of the booth. "That was one time. He hasn't done anything since, even though Martin and his mom are there every damn day." His jaw grew hard, he pursed his lips and looked away across the restaurant. Our coffee still hadn't come, and I wished for something to hold, wrap my fingers around to warm them, though I wasn't the least bit cold.

"You know it was an accident, right?" I said. "Even Angela knows that. And Martin. They don't blame you at all. No one does."

"I was driving. If I wasn't James would be fine. None of this would have happened." He looked at me, his eyes darkening, not with anger but with a desperation to be believed and understood. I understood. More than he knew, though he must have known on some visceral level, because he had sought me out.

I leaned forward in the booth and said, "My husband died because of me."

Although there were days, weeks even, when I managed to forget, there was also a kind of perverse pleasure in rehashing it, reminding myself that I had not been there when I was most needed, that I had failed to accomplish a small task that might have bought us some more time. So I told Jay the whole story. I was prepared as always for the listener to deny the facts, to placate and reassure me. But Jay just listened and then reached across the table to hold my hand. It felt strange, this near-stranger holding on to me, yet it felt right, too. We were comrades. We both had done grave damage, and no one outside our tiny circle could understand that. When our coffee arrived, we sipped in silence. We'd formed some secret bond, there was nothing more to say.

The dorm filled with noise. Luggage thumping down the hall, laughter, girls' high-pitched chatter, doors slammed by the wind, water running, toilets flushing. I sat in my room with the door closed and took a deep breath. It was summer, time for the next phase of my job, which was to chaperone, advise, lead tours and seminars. Like a somewhat more cerebral camp counselor, I would need to be vibrant, entertaining, and focused as I coached the students on college life. They would inhabit the dorms and cafeterias, and in classrooms keep up their studies and tutoring. The seniors would explore a typical college curriculum without the pressure—a kind of dress rehearsal. Their free time would be filled with movies, Frisbee, and jaunts to the lake. It sounded exhausting.

In years past, I'd always coordinated the summer program, hired tutors and teachers, arranged for transportation and field trips—but never lived on campus. I left that to college student staff, who were younger and single. It was a relief to leave the kids after a full day and relax with Dill on our porch chaise, eating salsa with chips and drinking white wine or sangria. "What a day," I would say invariably, lying against his chest, trying not to dribble food on myself. Once I added, "I could never do this full-time," and Dill corrected, "You *do* do this full-time." And I said, "Yes, but at least I can come home at the end of the day. I would die if I had to stay in the dorm with them like some old den mother."

And now, here I was, living in the dorm, about to be immersed in the life of high-school students twenty-four hours a day.

"Miss Rainey?" a voice called through my door. I stood and opened it. It was Sheena, sixteen with the eyes of a weary thirty-year-old. She also had a pierced eyebrow and the tattoo of a black hawk on her bare shoulder. Sheena favored tank tops almost year-round. In the winter, she wore oversize sweaters that fell off her shoulders, as if the bird needed air. I asked her once if there wasn't an age requirement for acquiring tattoos, and she assured me she had her mother's permission. In fact, her mother had accompanied Sheena to the tattoo parlor and had gotten her own, a large rose on the curve of her backside. "She's way too old for that sort of thing, but her latest boyfriend likes it," Sheena had said.

I asked her if she needed something. I opened the door wider. "Do you want to come in?"

Sheena sighed. "I don't know. I mean, I don't know if this is gonna work out."

"What?"

"This," she said, waving an arm expansively around the hallway. "This whole kids-at-camp routine. It's not for me. No offense," she added, glancing around my obviously lived-in surroundings.

"Well," I said. "This is your first summer here, right? Maybe you just need to give it some time. You've been here, what, thirty minutes?"

"Twenty," she said, implying that was plenty.

"Listen, I promise you, it won't be a waste of time. No one will treat you like a little kid, and you'll learn a lot. This is a *college,* remember?"

"Yeah, yeah. I guess." Sheena leaned into my threshold. "I just can't stand it when girls *giggle.* You know what I mean? It's like cats screeching. I *hate* it."

I had to admit, I knew what she meant. I never had been a joiner growing up, was always the quiet one hanging back at raucous slumber parties. I didn't pledge a sorority, and I eschewed bridal showers, Tupperware parties, and even gym memberships. It was because, I once realized, I loathed situations where I would overhear gossip among grown women who sounded exactly the same as sixth graders. "Well, she said," and "You won't believe this," and "I'm sorry, but that is just bizarre." And then the shrill cackling. So, I understood Sheena's resistance to the clubby atmosphere of a girls' dorm, even as I now lived in it myself.

I smiled at her. "If it gets to you, you can come camp out here with me. I promise: I never giggle."

She laughed at that. "I know," she said.

With doors opening and closing and glimpses of life spilling into the open, I learned almost by osmosis which girls were getting along and which were coming close to homicide; who was in love, and who was a virgin (fortunately, a few more girls that I'd expected); who craved order and who thrived on chaos; who was serious about her future and who was "still playing." Some of the girls dressed up for classes each day, with carefully pressed skirts, lined lips, and curled lashes, while others threw on shorts and dashed out at the last minute, eating hard bagels or potato chips on the way.

I had to navigate the bathroom now, watching for a break in the rush to the shower stalls, trying to find a slice of time when I might be alone, or nearly, at the row of sinks. Though I knew all of the girls in the program, I felt like the new kid at an orphanage, trying to fit in while wanting to crawl off and hide. Sheena was the one who, for some reason, elected herself my guide.

"No one's up before seven-thirty," she noted helpfully one morning when she spotted me checking the bathroom for crowds. "I know because I always wake up early to pee and no one's ever around. So, if you want to be alone, I suggest you set your alarm for, like, seven-fifteen." I nodded, impressed by her insightfulness. I wanted Sheena to plan my whole day for me, tell me when and what to eat ("You eat way too much cereal," I imagined her saying. "Have a blueberry muffin with butter, it'll do you good"). She was a cheerful cynic, my favorite kind, and the more she hung around my room, the more I liked her.

One night, when everyone else was at a mixer in one of the large common rooms, Sheena knocked on my door. "You in there?" she called, her now-familiar greeting. I opened the door and let her in.

"Why aren't you at the dance?" I asked. I knew she had a crush on one of the older boys, Sean, and we had laughed over their names, which made a kind of jaw-clamped tongue twister, Sheena and Sean, Sheena and Sean.

"Too corny," she said, shrugging. "All those girls lined up whispering, hoping someone will ask them to dance, like it's the nineteen fifties or something. Some of them, like Marisol, will just grab some guy and go shake her booty, but she's the exception to the rule."

I laughed. "Aren't you?"

"Naw. I mean, I'd dance, of course. I just don't like those organized things. Balloons and streamers and all that shit."

"You're just a nonconformist," I remarked.

"Right."

"Well, I was about to have some chips and salsa, if you'd care to join me."

"I would. Care," she said, deadpan. Sheena enjoyed mocking my polite grammar. She sat on the carpet beside me and dipped a chip into the bowl, tasted it, and then made a face. "You call that salsa? What is this garbage?" She looked at the jar on top of my tiny fridge and grimaced again. "Girl, you cannot buy store-brand crap and call it salsa. That's an insult to my race."

"Your race?" I laughed. Sheena was a dirty blond with green eyes smudged by dark kohl; her last name was Williams.

"Well," she said, leaning back against the bed. "I'm half Mexican, you know. This is fake," she said, pulling up a handful of light hair. "My dad was Waspy but, like, the black sheep of his family, mostly because he married my mother, Margarita Jimenez. And by the way, my mother makes the *best* salsa. I'll bring you some."

I thanked her and ate a chip, plain, and we sat in amiable silence for a few moments. Then I asked, "Sheena, what happened to your father?" Only her mother's name was on Sheena's initial application; I hadn't thought to ask why before.

She sighed, as if this question were routine by now. "He got hit by a car. On purpose." She glanced at me, then went on, tugging at the cuff of her blue jeans, pulling off little loose threads. "I was twelve years old, and we—my sister and brother and me—were staying at my

99

grandma's house for a week to give my mom a break. My dad had been off work on sick leave, but I found out later his sickness was depression. He just lay in bed all the time, and I thought he had some terrible illness. Well, I mean, he did. That night, maybe because he knew we wouldn't be home and my mother was at the store or something, he just got up out of bed and walked about a mile and a half to the highway and stepped right in front of a car. Some poor guy in a big Chrysler who didn't have time to stop or swerve just hit him at sixty miles an hour. My mom told her relatives it was an accident, because suicide is taboo in her family, in her religion, but eventually she told us kids the truth."

I didn't know what to say. It occurred to me that tragedy was all around—or else I simply attracted its victims now that I was part of the club. I reached over and took Sheena's hand, felt her fingers with all their silver rings folded into my palm. She leaned over and rested her head on my shoulder, her black hawk pressed against my arm.

"It's weird, isn't it?" she said softly.

"What is?"

"That when someone dies, they're just gone, completely gone, but when you talk about them, it's like they're out there somewhere." She lifted her head but kept holding my hand. "Every time I talk about my dad, I can see him clear as day, what he wore, how he stood, his voice, his hair parted on the side."

"I know what you mean," I said. "My husband is like that, too. I can still see him." I didn't tell her that, when I did, sometimes I wanted not to rush toward the image but to turn away.

"But you know he's really *gone*, right?" she said then, and I didn't know if she was challenging me and my sanity or needed reassurance for her own doubts. I nodded. Sheena pulled her hand away from mine, gently, and folded her fingers together like a little church, her index fingers the steeple. She opened the "door" and peered inside. "Every-one's there, praying," she said quietly. "You know, I still can't look in my parents' room, where he slept when he was sick, before. If my mother and her boyfriend leave the door open in the morning, I always shut it. It's like—I don't want to know for sure that he's not in there, sleeping, you know? Isn't that dumb? It's been *years*." She laughed derisively.

"It's not dumb at all," I said. I haven't been home since my hus-band died, I thought. I stood up, folded the cellophane bag of chips, screwed the lid onto the errant salsa, and placed it in the fridge. "You should go see Sean," I said, turning back to her. "At least for one dance. It would do you good."

Sheena laughed and stood up. "All right, all right. I'll go." At the door she smiled. "See ya later."

"Have fun," I called, like a mother watching her daughter going out on a Friday night. Suddenly I thought of Sheena's mother, with her boyfriend and her rose tattoo, and thought, Look what *she's* been through. But at least she has someone to curl up with at night, some-one to shove away the ghosts. I turned on my Tinker Bell light and stared into the darkness surrounding its glow.

Toward the end of the six weeks, my staff arranged for a daylong ferryboat trip along Lake Michigan and through smaller inland lakes and channels. The students were thrilled, and many had never been out so far on the lake before, only waded or swum near shore. On the ferry, armored with an orange life vest, I felt more comfortable staring into deep water. The captain, a sunburned man named Tommy, alerted me to the fact that, while he kept plenty of safety vests onboard, only small children were required to wear them. I thanked him and tied my canvas straps while my students grinned and snickered. Even placid Jillian, my boss, couldn't suppress a laugh.

The day was bright, the sky flat and blue as colored paper, and the water, fortunately was calm. I sat on the upper deck—the furthest from the water, and also the best viewing platform—and tilted my face toward the sunshine. Though summer was in full swing, I had spent little time outside and suddenly thought how much I had missed, working inside my office, the campus buildings, my little dorm room. It was time I paid attention to life around me again, to the simple things like fresh air and the slap of a paddle wheel in water.

I opened my eyes and peered back over the railing toward the engine house, and saw Tommy smiling at me through his glass lookout. He waved, but then I realized he was miming drowning, arms frantically thrashing the air. Ha ha, I thought. I really wasn't hydrophobic; I just knew my limits, and like many people with irrational fears, I simply avoided situations where mine might be tested.

"It's a *ferry*boat," Sheena said helpfully, eyeing my orange vest. "It goes about four miles an hour, and I don't think we could tip over if we wanted to."

"I know," I said. "I just would rather be safe than sorry."

"I hate to tell you, but you look pretty sorry." She laughed.

"How old are you?" I asked.

"Still sixteen," she said.

"Are you having fun?" I asked her. I noticed that in large groups she tended not to mingle but to drift around alone, or near me. It seemed that things between her and Sean hadn't progressed much. At the moment, he was standing at the railing, inches from a pretty girl named Lissa. Sheena watched them for a moment, rolled her eyes, and looked pointedly in the other direction.

"Yep, I'm having a ball," she said. "Couldn't be better."

"It's not that bad, is it? I mean, it's a perfect day. It's nice to be out, away from classes and everything." I leaned back and folded—or tried to—my arms over my puffy orange chest. I decided that maybe I didn't need so much protection and loosened the ties. I could hardly even tell we were moving unless I looked at the passing scenery. When I glanced over at Sheena, I saw that she was biting a hangnail with remarkable vigor. She paused, examined her nail, then tucked her hands under her armpits as if to prevent any more violence. Then she said dully, "Yeah. It's a goddamn beautiful day."

"Hey," I said a little sharply. We had a rule about profanity, and it applied to everyone, even my teacher's pet.

"Sorry," Sheena said, standing up suddenly, her bad mood like a cloud drifting with her. "I'm gonna walk around awhile."

Watching her wind her way along the upper deck, head down, I felt a little remorseful for chiding her. She had a lot on her mind; all the kids did at this time of the summer, everything coming to a close, real life about to resume. They would return home to families who likely would embrace them yet not understand fully what they had been through for six weeks, might not note the subtle maturity that had blossomed beneath their surfaces, might miss the fact that they'd had a taste of college life and weren't quite ready to regress.

A boy named Cyril strode past me, stopping to lean over the railing. Unlike Martin, who was outgoing and outspoken, Cyril rarely spoke unless spoken to; there were rumors among the others that he was gay, though they didn't harass him. There was something urgent and wizened about his expression that prompted a person to start conversations, to open the door for him to say what was on his mind.

"So, what did you think of college life?" I asked him.

Cyril turned and smiled, thinking. Then he said, "I had no idea there could be so much so close by."

"What do you mean?"

"I mean, I live about six blocks from this campus, and I used to think college was for geniuses. But when I sit in the science lab, you know, and study that table of elements, it makes perfect sense to me. And then I think inside those little symbols, like for nitrogen or magnesium or uranium, there are all these tiny universes. And inside cells and things so small you can't see without a microscope. And I feel, I don't know—so *full*, like I can get inside those worlds, too, and discover things." He paused, almost breathless, glancing quickly away.

"So, are you going to be a scientist?" I asked.

He smiled shyly. "Geneticist."

"I'm sure you'll be a great one."

Cyril leaned back over the rail and began tossing bread crumbs to a swath of seagulls following us like a tattered sail. I stood up and joined him; without a word he handed me a heel of bread from a plastic bag.

I thought about what lay over the horizon for Cyril and the other kids, just out of our vision, the way the deep blue line of Lake Michigan curved against the sky and led onward to Chicago and Milwaukee and hundreds of miles and unseen places beyond. And for the first time in many days nights weeks and months, I had the jarring, happy thought that perhaps what lay ahead was not just full of sorrow. "Tiny universes" were out there, ready to be discovered, one molecule at a time, one moment at a time.

Just as they had arrived, herded through the corridors, the girls in my dorm noisily moved back out. It was not a sad farewell, as I would be seeing most of them again in a month, when school and the regular Upward Bound sessions resumed, but I was melancholy nonetheless. A few of them came to give me hearty hugs and to tell me to "have a nice summer," as if I were one of them, a girl at camp.

Finally, Sheena tapped on my open door and stood there smiling. "Well," she said. "You're finally gonna get your peace and quiet back. And all the showers, right?"

"Yes," I said, laughing. "Now I can run naked up and down the hallway like I used to."

She regarded me skeptically for a moment, wondering whether to fall for it. I supposed she knew I was odd enough at times that it was not an inconceivable idea. "Well, have fun," she said, then paused. "And thanks for listening and all that."

"Any time," I said. I came to the door. "Want me to walk you out?" She nodded. When we got to the main door, I saw that Sean was there waiting. He grinned unabashedly at Sheena, who turned to me and shrugged as if to say, It's nothing, really. But I could tell by the way she returned his smile, she was more smitten than she dared let on.

"See you later, Miss Rainey," she said. *"Anna."* She laughed.

"You can call me Anna," I told her. Why not? I thought. She'd been more of a friend to me than anyone else lately, and I knew I would miss her curled up on the floor of my dorm room.

When she was gone, I walked back inside, struck by the silence. I had been leaving my door ajar so the students would feel welcome to drop in, but now that they were gone, I felt strangely vulnerable and alone. I closed the door and locked it. Then I wondered what to do, who to call. It seemed I had to see someone, preferably an adult for a change. I picked up the phone and dialed a number, surprising myself as much as the person on the other end of the receiver.

At nine o'clock, I waited at the main door. I knew the entry light silhouetted me to anyone passing by, but I wanted him to see me there when he came. Then, if he chose to, he could change his mind and keep walking. So, when he did come, I stepped back and watched him stride up the sidewalk, feeling a strange flutter in my stomach. It was as if I were once again a college student, a mere girl in her dorm waiting for her date. He smiled and pulled at the door handle. It was locked, so I pushed it open and he brushed in past my arm.

"I brought pizza," Jay said, holding a flat box on one palm.

"Great," I said. "We can eat it here." I waved toward the common room, where there were four sofas and a large TV. Jay sat down and placed the pizza on a square coffee table covered with discarded fashion magazines. He picked up a *TV Guide* and read the dates. "This is from last December," he said, laughing. "It looks like the Charlie Brown special is on."

"I wish," I said.

"Is that your favorite?"

"Well, that and Rudolph. I've seen that a hundred times. When I was little, only one family in our neighborhood had color TV, and we would all go over there and watch *Rudolph* and eat popcorn. It was a big event." Suddenly I was embarrassed, revealing my age in this way, as if I'd said we rode in a horse-drawn wagon to church. I knew when Jay was born there was no such thing as black-and-white television anymore.

He just laughed and handed me a paper plate he'd thoughtfully brought, along with cups and a bottle of cola. "I should have brought wine, I guess," he said, as if it had just occurred to him. He seemed a little nervous, uncertain. I wondered again if it had been a mistake to call him.

"This is fine," I said, taking a sip and wishing it *were* wine, or vodka. We ate the pizza, slice after slice, and watched a silly made-for-TV movie about a woman with a split personality and a confused spouse. She wore excessive makeup and delivered stilted lines such as "You don't know me at all." Her equally wooden partner answered that no, he didn't. And then he proceeded to find a lover with secrets of her own. It was confusing and awful, and Jay and I laughed and mocked the actors, guessed at the plot twists, and finally gave up and switched the television off.

He asked me about myself, then, and I considered telling him, carefully choosing an eclectic list of interests. I could tell him that psychology was my college major though I'd also flirted with studying music just because I wanted to hide out in the warm practice rooms, and fantasized about playing Vivaldi in a long black gown; that I loved buying books—sometimes just for the cover art; that I wasn't athletic but liked the sensation of speed and tried to be a runner, until I broke my wrist at the finish line; that I grew up an only child and so got used to needing only a little companionship, happy with one or two best friends, happiest when I married. I could tell him how much I hated the sight of married couples now, and how I had an impulse to shove them apart when they walked hand in hand past me.

I said none of these things aloud, of course. "What about you?" I said, to change the subject.

He shrugged. "Not so much to tell. What you see is what you get." He laughed a little. Then he said, "My real name is Jesús, but in Spanish, you know, there's no *j* sound, it's an *h*. So when I was two and my parents moved us to the States, they wanted to give me an American name. So they called me Jay. The funny thing is my mother's accent is still thick as mud so she calls me Hay."

I laughed. "What else?" I asked.

"I'm a roofer, I work fifty hours a week usually. Play baseball on Friday nights—usually." Jay smiled.

"Sorry you had to miss that," I said. "You didn't have to say yes when I called."

"Yes, I did," he said. He stared at me then, into my eyes as if willing me to read his thoughts, and I had to look away after a moment. Jay stood up and said, "Can you show me your room?" It was a quiet, curious request.

"Okay," I said, and led him down the dark hallway to the stairs, where I became keenly aware of the sound of his footsteps behind me. I opened the door on the second landing and led him through. "It's down here, in the middle," I said. "I could take any room I wanted, and I didn't want to be on the end. I'm not sure why." I turned my key in the only closed door and then stood inside.

"Charming, isn't it?" I laughed. There was my dresser with my few clothes, the small fridge humming soundlessly, the narrow bed with my sleeping bag and pillow.

"You really live here?" Jay asked, and I detected a note of concern.

"For now," I said, shrugging. "I kind of move around lately, and I wanted to be here for the summer program. The kids moved out this afternoon."

"Oh," he said, nodding, as if it made perfect sense.

"It's been a little too quiet since then," I added.

"Yeah, I bet," he said absently. Then he sat down on my bed and ran a hand through his black hair, looked around again, then up at me.

I slipped off my shoes, out of habit, but stood still. Jay waited. I knew what would happen next—it seemed that I had known all along, from the moment he'd walked into my dorm, and even before, at the coffee shop, and before, in my car. Now I went and sat beside him on my sleeping bag. There was no light except the moonlight slicing through the curtains. He lay down, pulling me gently with him, our bodies lined up on the bed barely big enough for us both. Leaning up again, he kissed my cheeks, my forehead, the tip of my nose, my lips. He smelled like fresh air. I thought of him walking, all the time, mornings to work, then home, to the store, across town under arches of maples and through rain and sunshine. It was as if he were part of the elements, a breeze blown into my lonely room. He gently pulled loose the elastic band holding back my hair, letting the curtain fall down around my face, and his. Then he moved down and kissed my throat, turning loose the buttons of my shirt. I held my breath, then sighed. His strong, callused fingers grazed my body, and every nerve ending rose to meet him, his body soft and hard, the pleasant earthy scent, the weight of his thighs on top of mine. Every thought and doubt I had was pushed away like the layers of our clothes, shoved free and dropped to the floor, forgotten. There was no past, no future. There was only now and breath and skin and soft steady rhythm. And afterward, slow silent tears. But this time, I did not lie alone brushing them away, turning to the wall and the solace of sleep. This time someone wiped my wet cheek, said, Shh, and kissed my eyelashes. This time someone wrapped himself around my loneliness and stayed until a new day filled the room.

It was a one-night stand, I told myself, awful as it sounded. Then it happened again, the next night and the next. Like a shoplifter, I slipped them into my pocket and justified my actions: it meant nothing;

it didn't hurt anyone; no one would ever know. I thought of Dill, imagined him sitting sadly in the dark corner watching me, like a boy not chosen at the dance. Or worse, scowling. Another time I thought I was simply dreaming, the dream within the dream where I was making love to a stranger while my husband watched, and then I realized that my husband was dead; none of it could be real.

On the third night I contemplated the notion of sex without love: it once had been incomprehensible to me. I'd marveled at the idea of someone peeling off her clothes for a man, touching, being touched, doing all of those strange and tantalizing things with someone she did not love. Now, suddenly, I understood how one could do it: it could be just the desperation of a numb body craving sensation. No different, in a way, than the hot shock of whiskey on a tongue, or the startling feeling of an ice cube pressed against a thigh on a warm day, or the melting of tired muscles onto a soft bed, with snow pummeling the window outside. All of them different but welcome sensations. Like Jay's body pressed against mine, skin on skin. I craved and needed him, even though I hardly knew him and, of course, didn't love him. But it was better to sleep with a near-stranger, I reasoned, than with someone I did know and care about, like Philip. Besides, Jay beside me eased the pain we both carried; exhausted by guilt and grief, we needed something else for a change. Something good. Something shocking.

I woke one night, startled to find him in my bed, as if in my sleep I had forgotten what we'd done. I didn't want to disturb him, so I slipped out and quietly made my way, naked, down the hall to the bathroom. The door echoed behind me in the long tiled room, and I didn't bother turning on the light. It was so dark that I had to feel my way along the walls, the cool metal of the stalls, and then the ridged tiles of the showers. I reached for the faucet and turned on the water, hot as I could stand, and then I stood there, weeping, convulsing. My body shook with sobs and I knew that the sound reverberated off the walls, but I was far enough away I was sure Jay couldn't hear me. No one could, and there was such emptiness in that thought, I simply gave myself up to it, pressed myself against the warm wet tiles and stayed there until I no longer felt a thing, as if I had become part of the water flowing over me, as if I were melting away and would slide down the drain, nothing left.

One morning the phone rang beside my ear when the sun was still thin and wan, barely stretching over the far trees. When I lifted it and mumbled a greeting, Martin's voice shouted, "He's back! He's back! You have to come see him you won't believe it!" I sat upright and tried to slow him down. *Whoa, whoa.* Then I began to understand. It was James. Little sleeping beauty James, who had dozed away three quarters of his ninth year, grown an inch while in his bed, and also sprouted a new tooth—all of a sudden, as if a magic wand waved across his rehabilitation room, he had woken up and smiled. Angela, Martin reported, hyperventilated and fainted on the floor. But now they were celebrating; it had happened in the wee hours, and Martin just had to tell someone. Someone, I thought, was me, and I was flattered to be the chosen one.

"I tried to call Jay," Martin went on, "but he wasn't home." My heart sank a bit at that, and then I blushed, though Martin couldn't possibly have imagined that Jay was asleep beside me, curled under the sleeping bag we had turned into a double-size cover.

After I promised Martin I would come to the hospital in a while, I shook Jay a little, shoving his shoulder, curved and brown where the cover had slipped away. I had no desire to kiss or caress it; that was for the darkness, when our need and lust swept through us. In the morning we resumed our old selves, protective, solemn, self-deprecating. We dressed quietly, and if one bumped into the other, we murmured, "Sorry."

"Hey," I said now.

"Hm," he mumbled without opening his eyes. Then he turned to look at me. "Oh," he said, "I thought you were my mother calling me."

"No, it's me." *He still lives with his mother.*

"Who calls so dang early?"

"James," I said. "That was Martin calling about James. He woke up, Jay, he's fine." Then I added his brother's elated words, "He's back."

Jay sat upright, covers falling away like water; in a moment he was standing on solid ground, pulling on his clothes, asking me over and over if it were true. "Are you *sure*?" he asked. I nodded, tears in my eyes. It was the first time in my life I had felt a miracle blowing through close enough to feel its power, like a strange weather pattern, something no one dared believe could happen, happening. Shaking a little, I got dressed, too.

"Let's go see him," I said.

Jay beamed. His whole countenance had changed, the light of sheer relief shining through his skin.

When the elevator doors opened, we could see a cluster of nurses and other hospital staff grinning and laughing, peering into the room from the corridor, then dispersing, talking animatedly. I hesitated, pushed Jay ahead of me.

"You go on," I said. "I think I'll just wait outside. I don't want it to look like we came together."

He grinned, then went in, tentatively, though on springy feet. I lagged behind, then inched close enough to see into the room so I could watch the drama unfold, a little unrehearsed play for my singular enjoyment.

Martin was blowing up colored balloons, knotting the ends, and then rubbing them softly on his brother's head, where they clung like giant grapes. James was laughing. Sitting up in his immaculate bed—the sheets no longer taut and still but a rumpled heap on his lap—James was fully and utterly alive. His dark eyes sparkled, though he looked vaguely sleepy, and his wiry arms waved around as he tried to catch the balloons drifting past. Angela sat on a chair pulled all the way to the side of the bed, and she was leaning way in, her hand firmly on her little boy's leg, then moving down the shin, caressing, then pinching his toes playfully. She looked up when she saw Jay in the doorway, and her smile was enormous, a billboard for unswerving faith—*See, I told you!*

Jay stood there for a long moment at the periphery, then walked forward, shook Martin's outstretched hand, then Angela's—though she lunged up and hugged him—and finally, like the doubter at the tomb, he reached out and touched James's hand, patted his knobby shoulder. "Hi, sport," he said, his voice cracking with emotion.

Feeling suddenly like a voyeur, I backed away and headed for the elevator. Let them be alone, I thought reverently. I resolved to call later and congratulate the family on their happy moment. But there was another, sickly nagging feeling, as if I'd taken the wrong medication. What was it? I wondered, dumbfounded at myself and my capacity for disenchantment; couldn't I look at the bright side for once, the silver lining, the pinpoint of light at the end of the tunnel and simply be grateful? Obviously James was fine. His mother had prayed and hoped and waited in the darkness—as had Martin, and Jay—and finally been rewarded.

And there it was, plain as day, as the elevator and my spirits plunged downward. I was jealous, deeply, bitterly, irrationally jealous: I had prayed and hoped and waited, too. Where was *my* light, my reward?

W here did you go?" Jay asked on the phone. It was getting dark, the sky over the trees and the battered tennis courts was smudged a soft purple, clouds dragged through the last streaks of sunlight, leaving them gilt-edged. I wondered how many people driving home from work bothered to notice it. Probably few. Probably only small, worn-out children, pausing underneath sprinklers, shivering a little, looking up and marveling at the stunning summer sky.

Jay was waiting for an explanation. "Martin asked about you, and I said I thought you were coming—I didn't tell him you were already there, because of what you said, about us. But they really wanted to see you." He paused. "So do I."

You can't, I thought into the receiver. But I said, "I just thought you needed time alone with them."

"Well, God knows, it's like a huge burden has fallen off me, you know? But I still wish you'd been there, Anna. And Martin would think it was cool—about us, I mean."

It was worse than I thought. He'd said it again, *us*. It was as if we had been to the same movie but seen different versions. I felt like a girl again, breaking up with a boyfriend and trying to do so magnanimously. It's not you, it's me.

"Jay," I said softly, then loud enough for him to hear, "Jay. This— thing, between us. It just happened. Like your accident, it was no one's fault, no one saw it coming." *Liar.* "And it served a purpose for both of us for a little while, a kind of comfort. But it can't, we can't go on like that anymore." There, I had said it. I worked the zipper of my sleeping bag up and down nervously. It really had been an accident, I thought, though we both drove into it with our eyes open, goading the crash, wanting the impact. But we couldn't stay lying in the wreckage forever; couldn't he see that?

"So, that's that, the end? Is that what you're saying?" His words sounded so choked I almost took it all back.

"Things will go back to normal for you now," I said.

"What are you talking about? And what makes you think you can decide for me what my life will be like? Don't I have a say in it?"

"Jay, I'm a widow. I'm thirty-five years old. I can't just go around dating twenty-year-olds because I'm lonely. It isn't right. It isn't fair to you, either."

"I'm twenty-one," he corrected. "Consenting adult. And I don't care about how old I am or you are. I never cared about that. I saw you, not a number."

Apparently, he didn't understand. For a short time we were in the same pit, facing the same impossible obstacles, our looming guilt, our terrible crimes. But in one sweep his had been erased; the child woke and walked. Jay was redeemed and set free; I was still pacing around below.

"I just need to be alone," I said. "I'm sorry." I set the phone into its cradle and turned back to watch the sky slowly bruise.

In August, with three weeks left until the college semester com-
menced, I had to make other plans, find a new nest. After living
alone all summer, I didn't want to go back to staying with friends, and
besides, I didn't want to seem desperate, incapable. It was time to start
carving out a niche for myself, a real home of some sort. I daydreamed
about what that might be—a tiny cottage on a precipice of a Mediter-
ranean island (a widow's peak, I joked to myself); a tree house with
rope ladder and screens all around, a lovely idea while the weather was
warm; or perhaps a smart efficiency apartment in Chicago or New
York—maybe it was time for me to move on altogether, start over as a
different person in a different city.

But short-term thinking was the best I could manage, and all I
could bring myself to do was walk to the small bookstore in town and
scour the bulletin board for rentals. I needed to find something cheap;
the bank was continuing to deduct mortgage payments from my account each month. Whenever I balanced the checkbook I would swallow hard, subtracting that solid number. I had pinched here and there
to save money, hadn't really bought much of anything in months except for food and necessities, the camping gear, and one day on impulse, a silver pen. Later it occurred to me that it was just like one Dill
used to have and misplaced. He often lamented losing that pen, and I
had planned to buy him a new one but forgot. Suddenly, in a store, I
found myself reaching for the pen a split second before a signal to my
brain reminded me that Dill no longer needed it. But I did. Now I
kept the pen deep in my purse, never using it but aware that it was
there.

The bookstore was quiet. Staff people tucked new hardcovers onto shelves, straightened wilting displays of "beach reading," and talked to each other about their weekend plans and love lives. I eavesdropped for a while: *God, he's so stubborn, which isn't so bad all the time, if you know what I mean. . . . I got this really cute red thing, you know, clingy top, flared just a little at the bottom, and I can't wait to wear it. . . . Yeah, he said he made reservations for Saturday and Sunday and if I can get off Monday, too. . . . I'd give anything to lose ten or fifteen pounds, but he says he likes me "rounded."* I marveled at this other kind of life going on around me, everywhere, probably. When I was married, and before that, dating, I was never very good at fashion small talk, and felt it a kind of betrayal to spill nighttime secrets with girlfriends. But I had taken for granted, like the store clerks, that I was loved by a man, that he wanted me, that if I put on a new dress we both got a charge out of it.

I concentrated on the notices tacked before me. Only two looked promising: a second-floor apartment in the historic district ("All utilities included, gabled windows, leafy view"—I appreciated the poetic choice of words), and a two-room rental above the music shop. The latter was tempting, the idea of waking to guitar tuning and keyboards. However, the owner also sold drum sets, and I knew that preadolescents in particular liked to pop in just to try them out. I peeled off one of the dangling strips of paper with phone numbers for the first listing and started out the door.

"Anna," a voice behind me said. I turned and there was Jon Gordon, Jr. He was smiling tentatively, brows knit a little as if worried I might not remember him.

"Hi, Jon," I said. "How have you been?"

"Fine." He nodded. "What about you? You stopped coming to the group. I hope—I mean, I hope it wasn't because of me." He cleared his throat.

"No! Of course not."

"Well, that has bothered me for a while. That maybe I made you feel awkward about coming back."

I felt terrible that I had burdened him, but was also a tiny bit resentful that he thought I was that sensitive. "No, really. It just wasn't the right time for me to be there, talking about myself, you know? I guess it works for some people, but I had to trust my instinct."

He nodded again. "That's a good philosophy."

"I guess so." There was an uncomfortable pause, during which we both looked around as if hoping someone might come to rescue us from this accidental encounter.

Suddenly a young girl appeared at Jon's side and looked at us both. She was pudgy, her pink T-shirt taut over doughy belly, and her pale brown hair was pulled into a tight, unflattering ponytail that accentuated her puffy, flushed face. "Dad?" she said. "Are we going or what?"

This was the wan girl in Victorian laced nightgowns I had pictured curled into her little bed? Funny how quickly the mind fashions stereotypes. A child lost her mother, and I imagined someone small and fragile, a waif. Yet here she was, a robust, grumpy girl, solidly real.

"Celie, this is Anna—sorry, I forgot your last name," Jon said.

"Rainey," I said. "Anna Rainey. Nice to meet you, Celie."

She said nothing, offered no smile or acknowledgment. She turned to look up at her father once more. "Can we go, *please*?"

"Honey, we will in a minute. Please don't be rude," Jon said firmly, though I saw him wince a little, as if chiding his daughter pained him deeply. Yet, I admired that he seemed to be trying to treat her normally. Little as I knew about parenting, I felt pretty certain that even a suffering child still needed boundaries, expectations, the sense that life will go on nonetheless.

"Listen, I have to go, too," I said, wanting to offer the miserable child a way out. "It was nice to see you again," I said, meeting Jon's eyes. "I hope everything is going well for you."

Jon smiled a little. "Yeah, we're doing okay, thanks. Nice to see you, too, Anna."

When I pushed my way through the door, I heard Celie demand, "Who was that?" but I couldn't hear the response.

I t's a month-at-a-time lease," Mrs. Edie VanderWal informed me. "No offense, but it's how we keep tabs on renters, in case of problems. I'm sure you won't be a problem," she added quickly. She had glanced over my application and noted the box marked "married," crossed out, and the "widowed" square checked. It was the first time I had put it in writing. I knew she noticed, because she clucked her tongue and then gave me a careful, sympathetic glance.

"That's fine," I said, not telling Mrs. VanderWal that I never knew how long I might stay in one place. One month at a time sounded reasonable to me; I often had the sense of sailing toward the end of the earth, not fully convinced its surface was round. Any minute I might simply plunge over the edge. It was better not to make plans too far in advance.

"So, you may move in as soon as Saturday, if you'd like. It's been empty just for a couple of days, and Mr. VanderWal likes to give the walls a good whitewashing before a new tenant arrives."

I looked around. The entire apartment seemed to be in immaculate condition already. The windows gleamed, the maple trees just beyond pressing close enough to fill the room with a sunny greeny light. "I like the 'leafy view,'" I said cheerfully. Mrs. VanderWal gave me a quizzical look. I wondered if her husband had been the one to write the advertisement, or if she simply didn't remember her own wording. People sometimes were unexpectedly poetic. Once I bought a pound of ground sirloin at the local market and the elderly butcher told me I had "the eyes of a water nymph." I laughed and his eyes twinkled. Later, I wondered where he had gotten such an idea, if the words just came to him, out of nowhere.

"There's no shower curtain," Mrs. VanderWal was saying. "But I might have an extra downstairs—unless you want to buy one yourself. I don't think they're that expensive." Her tone was apologetic but hopeful. I thought it must be exhausting, looking after the needs of strangers all the time, even if they did pay you for your trouble.

"It's okay," I assured her. "I can pick one up before I move in." I handed her the first month's rent plus security deposit. She smiled, clearly relieved to see that I was already proving trustworthy. "You can just pull the door closed behind you when you go," she said. "Take all the time you want looking around."

When she was gone, I walked from room to room—there were three, bedroom, kitchen, living area. The bathroom was small, with lavender tiles and rings dangling from the bare, wraparound bar. Apparently the last occupant or occupants had ripped the shower curtain down before leaving; there were tufts of vinyl still attached to some of the rings. Perhaps it had happened in a fit of rage, or impatience or lust. There was no sign of abuse or neglect anywhere else in the apartment.

"Well," I said aloud to myself, wondering for a panicked moment how long I could sleep in my sleeping bag on the carpeted bedroom floor, and where I would sit to eat my meals. For the first time it struck me as ludicrous that I still owned a small houseful of very respectable and useful furniture. Dill and I were frugal but had a knack for unearthing inexpensive antiques at estate sales and Goodwill, though sometimes we splurged. Once, after he received a large bonus, we drove into Chicago and bought a red sofa, huge, overstuffed, overpriced. I loved burrowing into its curvy depths to watch action movies on a Friday night. Now, standing in my new empty living room, I felt a deep longing for it. All of it—the sofa, the house, the rugs, the television remote with the numbers almost rubbed off by Dill's twitching, the blue-rimmed dishes and silver candlesticks from our wedding, our books, framed photographs, our life all around me. But I knew I still couldn't face walking through that door, standing in those rooms, full of wonderful things but so totally lacking the one thing that mattered.

There were moments when I felt the polar opposite, when all I wanted was to drive home and run through the door, and take it all in. Force myself to look at Dill's things, our things. But somehow that seemed like a kind of surrender, as if by giving in to the urge to go back home, I would let death win. Dill, in his sudden departure, would win.

Lying awake in my new apartment, on the bed I had acquired through Rent-a-Room—along with a few other inexpensive basics: sofa, table, dresser, chair—but still nestled in my sleeping bag out of habit, I found myself thinking about Jay. *Jesus,* my temporary savior. I missed his youthful but slow and careful kissing, his strong hands on my body. Perhaps it was out of a need to obliterate my memories of Dill's body, but whatever the reasons, I relived Jay's caresses, the way he undressed me and complimented me by the light of my small lantern. I lamented cutting him off so abruptly. He had not called again, and I didn't blame him.

I got up and padded to my new kitchen—a revelation in a way, to have a whole kitchen again, not just a tiny fridge but a large Kenmore, a dishwasher, a gas range and oven. I wondered if I would start seriously grocery shopping again, cooking meals from scratch. Maybe I would have a dinner party. I turned the tap on and leaned down for a long drink. Standing in the dark kitchen, wiping the water from my mouth, I had a powerful urge to call Jay now, in the middle of the night, and beg him to come over. I would have to give him directions, explain that I had moved, and hope that the sound of my voice, my longing, would be enough to coax him to dress and rush right over, undress as soon as he arrived. I sat down, trying to decide if I dared.

I sat for a long time in the kitchen, drinking water—still so thirsty—watching the moisture trickle down the sides of the glass, a glass I had purchased in a meager set of four, along with two plates, microwave-safe, and a cereal bowl. All of my belongings could now fit into two boxes and two large duffel bags. Maybe this was a good way to live, like Thoreau, wasting little, wanting nothing. I'd learned to settle for small pleasures—a handful of cold, clean grapes, a piece of chocolate pie taken home from a restaurant in a Styrofoam triangle, fresh air through the window, sleep. I missed other things, like being touched. So I thought of Jay. I ran my finger around the rim of my glass as I considered. He might refuse to come, or even speak to me, but on the other hand, maybe he had just been waiting for me to change my mind. Maybe our meeting hadn't been accidental but fate throwing us together because we'd needed each other.

As my hand hovered near the telephone, I suddenly pulled it back. I knew it would be grossly unfair, using him like that. Thou shalt not, I thought ruefully. I didn't love Jay, and though he might have thought fleetingly that he loved me, I was sure he'd amended that feeling as soon as I hung up on him.

I went back to bed, folded my arms over my chest in a kind of self-defiance, and decided that I had been foolish to think any-thing was fate. Things happened—car accidents, aneurysms, children falling into and then out of comas, women and men meeting and break-ing apart—and all it amounted to was life, plain and simple, messy and unpredictable and completely random.

Three days later, I ran into Jon and Celie Gordon again. This time at the grocery store, where they were discussing the merits of various brands of cereal. I rounded the corner of the aisle and saw that Celie was holding up a box of frosted something-or-other and reading aloud the grams of sugar. Jon offered another box for debate. She shrugged and took his selection, tossed it into their cart. I hardly dared interrupt their cozy father-daughter exchange, but Jon spotted me lurking there and called out, "Anna Rainey!" which made me laugh, the fact that he remembered my last name and seemed so proud to shout it out, like a contestant on a quiz show. Celie turned then, too, and scowled a little, but then returned her face to its bland indiffer-ence.

"Hi, Jon, hi, Celie," I said, slowly pushing my cart near theirs. "What a surprise."

"Are you following us?" Celie blurted.

I laughed. "No," I said. "This is a sheer coincidence, I promise."

Jon ignored his daughter's tactlessness and smiled at me, glancing briefly into my cart, which held an optimistic amount of staples, as if I were prepared to cook for a soccer team. "I'm just setting up house," I said by way of explanation.

"Oh? Did you move?" Jon asked.

"Well, yes. I had to vacate my last—apartment. It's a long story.

Anyway. I better let you finish your shopping. See you later." I scooted past them, but Jon reached out and tapped my shoulder. His fingers latched there for a moment, as if he were attempting to reel me in.

"Sorry," he said, pulling his hand away. "I just wanted to say, if you aren't doing anything later, Celie and I were going to the skating rink. If you'd like to join us."

"Oh, I don't skate," I said quickly.

"Well, neither do I. Celie does." Jon placed his hand on his daughter's head, and she ducked away from it, turned to inspect a display of breakfast bars. Jon went on, tucking his hands in his pockets, "I just watch on the sidelines, drink some watery coffee."

There was something about his earnestness, and the spark of light in his sad blue eyes, that made me nod. "All right," I said. "What time?"

The arena was cold, like stepping inside a cooler. Only about a dozen skaters spun around the ice in colorful street clothes, though two young, lithe girls wore skirts and tights, their hair in braids that whipped the air when they twirled. I sat at a small rink-side table near the concession stand and waited for Jon to bring our coffee. While he was in line, I scanned the ice for Celie. She was still sitting on one of the wooden benches, tying on her skates. She wore pink again, obviously a favorite color, this time in a dress that was ill-fitting, with a flippy skirt. She was probably twenty-five pounds overweight for her age and height, and I worried that she would stumble when she stood up on her blades and tried to step into the rink. To my surprise, she did not step but glided onto the surface, and immediately raced once around the entire oval, passing skaters older and slimmer.

Then she turned, stopped herself with a quick sideways motion that sent sparks of ice from her blades. Pausing to look up, she spotted me at the table and waved. I was flattered by this show of attention, but then realized that Jon had come up behind me and was waving down to his daughter, a tray balanced in his other hand.

"Here," he said, setting it down. "I decided to get something to eat, too. I always get hungry after grocery shopping." I glanced down and saw coffee, milk, Danish, and an order of French fries. Jon laughed. "I didn't know if you'd like salty or sweet."

I took a Danish and poured a little milk into my coffee, turning it an ashy brown. "You were right about the coffee," I said. I put my elbows on the table, but it was too cold against my skin and I hugged myself a little. I hadn't prepared for the sudden indoor climate change. I turned to look at the skaters again and said, "Celie is really good. Does she take lessons?"

"She used to, but the instructor had back surgery and we haven't found another yet. We still come here once a week or so—it helps Celie feel calm, I think. You know, just lost in her own world out there."

I nodded. "Is she doing all right?" I asked.

"As well as you'd expect, I guess," he said. "She has a best friend, Martha, whom she can confide in, and that's important. And we get along, we've only really had each other for a long time." He paused, brushed a hand over his eyes, though there were no tears. Perhaps it was a nervous tic. "But school is another story. I dread it already, when she goes back in a few weeks. I've hired tutors, but nothing seems to help."

I said nothing for a moment, just pretended to drink. I dipped the Danish into my coffee, so that the sugary coating melted off into it. I stirred and tasted. A small improvement.

"What do you do, by the way?" Jon was asking, apparently attempting to change the subject. "I mean, when we were in the SOLO group, I'm sure you introduced yourself, and I'm sorry I don't remember what you said."

I laughed. "Probably nothing memorable." I remembered him saying that he was a photographer and that I'd been surprised, thinking he looked like a salesman or a banker. "I'm the academic coordinator and counselor for Upward Bound."

Jon's face brightened. "Really? You're a counselor? Maybe you could work with Celie."

"Well, she's too young for the program—it's for high-school students."

"Oh. Well, if I paid you, could you work with her, on the side?"

I hesitated. "I doubt she would be interested. She doesn't seem to like me very much."

"Well, don't take it personally. She isn't so bad, really. Just your average depressed, motherless preadolescent." He looked embarrassed and chagrined.

I felt I had to do something quickly. It was like seeing someone's sleeve in flames; you tossed cold water over it without even thinking. "I'll see what I can work out," I heard myself saying. "There's actually a lull right now, before the fall program starts. If you want, I could meet with her once or twice a week to see how it goes." The invitation for coffee had turned into something I hadn't envisioned. I merely had felt sorry for Jon and his morose child, didn't want to hurt his feelings again. I never expected to be lured into a relationship—with a ten-year-old girl.

"Dad! Watch this!" Her high, thin voice called from below. Jon and I both turned to see her race gracefully to the center of the rink and proceed to spin into a blur of pink and white. Her arms drove up and then out like a mechanical toy, and then she slowed to a perfect curtsy, drawing applause not just from us but from all the other people who had stopped in their tracks to watch. Celie, blushing, glistening with sweat, beamed. I saw for the first time that she had dimples on either side of her mouth when she smiled.

Lydia invited me to dinner at her house, with Lexi. "A reunion," she called it, although the three of us had never been a trio. Since Dill's death, though, the two of them seemed to have formed a kind of sisterhood that involved watching out for me. One or the other called me every other week or so, alternating, and I came to suspect that they had worked out a system: Your turn, I called her last week. She still seems okay, but I think we need to get together for an assessment. Let's have dinner.

It was a Friday night, and Lexi had arranged for Penny to stay at her father's house, though it wasn't his usual weekend for custody. Lexi had arrived at Lydia's before I did, though I arrived right at the scheduled time. I wondered if they had agreed to meet early, to present a unified front when I showed up.

"Hi! How are you?" Lexi called brightly as she opened the door. "I'm so glad to see you!" I hadn't noticed her propensity for speaking in exclamation points before and wondered what she had up her sleeve.

"Fine, thanks," I said. I came into the kitchen and set down the spinach salad I had brought with me. A simple thing, but I had spent an hour on it, so unaccustomed to food preparation, especially for more than one. I'd decorated it with carefully curlicued carrot slivers and bolts of red pepper, sprigs of cilantro.

"It's beautiful!" Lexi said.

"Yeah, it looks great," Lydia said, peeling off the cellophane wrap.

"It's just a salad," I said.

"So—" said Lexi.

"So—what?" I asked. "You seem awfully excitable," I told her. I was just waiting for one of them to drop the bomb: We've been worried about you, you need to get out more. It isn't healthy living alone, I know of a good shrink.

"Okay," Lexi said carefully. "The reason for this dinner is—"

"Wait," Lydia interjected. "Why don't we have some wine first?"

Oh, perfect, I thought, get me drunk, then start the intervention.

When three glasses of sparkling cold Chardonnay were poured, I frowned, but Lexi grinned and lifted her glass above her head. "A toast," she said merrily. Lydia lifted her glass, too, and laughed.

I looked from one to the other, bewildered. "What are we toasting, exactly?"

"My engagement, exactly!" Lexi shrieked.

"To Lexi and her new man, and her new life," Lydia said, clinking glasses all around. I almost shuddered with relief, embarrassed, too, for having let myself grow so self-centered. Other people's lives were going on, all the time, every moment. Somehow, when I wasn't looking, Lexi had met a man called George at a book group, and within weeks they were madly in love.

"So, what's he like?" I asked.

"He's a manager at the newspaper," Lexi said, "and he's funny, and sweet, and—I don't know. As soon as you see him, you just know he's a good guy."

"And he's hot," Lydia added.

"How do you know?" Lexi asked, laughing. "You haven't even met him yet."

"I just know," she said. "I can see it in your eyes."

We sat down around Lydia's familiar coffee table, on paint-stained pillows, and toasted again. We passed around a crumbly cheesecake, forgoing plates and digging in with our forks and fingers. When we leaned back on our pillows, sated, Lexi said, "Ain't life grand?" I saw Lydia glance quickly at me and then at Lexi. I saw the look and knew what she was thinking. I didn't want her to squelch the mood with anxiety over me, not for a minute.

"Yes," I agreed. "Life's grand." I wondered then for the first time if it really was possible to find love again, twice in one lifetime. But then, Lexi's first marriage had been a disaster from the beginning. Her ex-husband, Tom, had an affair with a co-worker days before the wedding, though he only confessed to it to Lexi two years later. And he had others, sporadically, like a recurring virus he couldn't seem to shake. Lexi had loved him but was continually "disappointed," as she understatedly put it. Perhaps with George, then, was the first time she had found the real thing. Perhaps there really was only one true love per person and I already had used up my quota. There was no use thinking about it anyway, I reasoned; this was Lexi's night, and I was supposed to be happy for her. And I was.

Of course, I had to keep my word, so Celie arrived at my office door promptly at three-thirty on a windy September Tuesday, stoic, silent, a faded canvas backpack hanging limply from one arm. Jon had called to tell me he wouldn't be able to bring her himself, that she would be getting a ride there from a friend's mother. When I saw her standing there, staring, nearly glaring, at me, I took a breath and made myself smile.

"Come on in," I said, sliding out of my chair to greet her, showing her to a seat beside my wide desk. I cleared away some papers so that she could set her books down. "What would you like to work on first?" I asked. Celie shrugged. I tried again. "What homework do you have today?" At this, Celie reluctantly unzipped her bag and yanked free a pile of books and a wrinkled loose sheet of paper scrawled with some illegible notes. Looking it over, I wondered if the child were more seriously learning disabled than her father realized or admitted.

"Is this your assignment sheet?" I asked. She nodded. "Can you read it to me?"

"It says pages thirty-three to thirty-seven," she said in a deeply bored tone. "In math. Five whole dumb pages."

I looked at the paper again, then asked cautiously, "Is this your handwriting?"

Celie shrugged again. "Yeah. But not my real writing. I did it left-handed because I was bored."

"Oh. Are you always bored in school?"

"Yes."

"Is there anything you like about it?"

"Going home. Saturdays. Vacation. Snow days—but we only had two last year."

The child was so determined to be unhappy, it was like a mission. She was ready to lash out at a cruel world. Her demeanor suggested, *Why bother? You will only get hurt anyway. You will only die.* I didn't know what I could do to help her, or even if I could help her simply conquer long division. I remembered someone in Joanne's group saying, "The way out of the ocean is one stroke at a time." I thought maybe I could help Celie learn that, even if I still was struggling myself. Blind leading the blind. It was worth a try.

"Do you have a pencil?" I asked.

"I guess."

"Can you get it out, then, so we can get started here?" I prodded patiently.

She dug around for one, seeing that I was not going to be dissuaded from the unpleasant task. She took a long time, inspecting an assortment of colored pencils, some with decorative erasers—a fat cloud, a soccer ball, a ladybug—and one with long, hairy strands of synthetic feathers. Then she took out a piece of paper, smoothed it over my desk, and still not meeting my eyes, began to copy the first problem from her book. There she stopped. I realized that all the preparations were delay tactics as she had no idea whatsoever how to begin. The numbers seemed to swim before her round, wounded eyes, and several times I saw her brush the flat of her hand over the page, as if to make them disappear.

"Okay," I said quietly, turning the book around to look at it myself. Then I took a separate piece of paper and began to break down the first problem. I showed her how the dividend was inside its little house, or shed, and the divisor outside it wanting to get in. All Celie had to do was "fit" the divisor into the dividend, the larger number, and that would be the key, the answer. She seemed to warm slightly to the metaphor, and I concluded that perhaps she was a quietly imaginative child who was just stifled by the rigid constraints of mathematics. If I could help her to see the beauty in numbers, though, perhaps she could take them into herself, make them real. Conquer her fear and her failings.

"Here," I said, "take the smaller number, sixty-four, and see how many times it fits into the big number, seven hundred sixty-eight. Start small." I leaned over my desk to show Celie how I was arriving at the solution, step by step. I sat back upright. "Twelve, that's the quotient. See? It's a perfect fit. Like new shoes."

Celie's chubby cheeks flushed, and she blinked, looked down at the paper. I didn't know what could possibly have upset her; the solution seemed crystal clear to me, and I went over it again, slowly, showing her how to check the answer by multiplying. Still she said nothing, just sat with her hands in her lap.

She looked at her feet, swirled them in circles around the carpet, then ran a finger over her lips, pressing hard the way a woman might to rub off lipstick. When she took her hand away, her lips had turned bright pink.

"My mother bought me these shoes when she was feeling better last fall. She was in remission," Celie blurted. She looked down at the shoes again, as if they might be magic somehow. "They don't really fit anymore, you know, I grow all the time. But I like them anyway." Her voice drifted off, as if she realized she had been speaking out loud. It was the most I had ever heard her say at one time.

"I'm sorry about your mother," I said quietly. "I really, really am. We can stop for now if you want to. I'll call your teacher and tell her we're working on this, and maybe she can give us a little extension on the assignment. Would that be okay with you?"

Celie nodded slowly, puffing out her cheeks with air, then holding her breath. The poor child was drowning. And I didn't have any idea how to help her keep her head up.

The fall semester had begun, bringing a new batch of students to the Upward Bound classrooms. I greeted them all the first day, and in turn introduced them to their college tutors. But I had a hard time keeping their names straight, even though I had recruited them the previous spring, when they were in the eighth grade. Some of them smiled at me in recognition, but they were strangers to me; I realized we had met when I was still in the fog of early grief, going through the motions, doing my job but not really connected to it. I decided I would have to memorize them, and soon they would be as familiar to me as Sheena and Martin and Marisol and all the others. Yet, for some reason, I had no energy for them; I felt like a mother whose children are finally nearly ready to leave the nest, who finds herself saddled with a new brood of needy infants. It was always like this, every fall, the kids coming in shy and green, me holding their hands for the first months and showing them the way. But I had never resented it before.

I wondered if it had anything to do with Celie and my failure to help her. She came twice a week after school, and I attempted to tutor her for one hour during my own students' tutoring sessions, when normally I would be doing paperwork or taking an afternoon coffee break. We sat and labored over the stubborn numerals that resisted dividing like cells under a microscope; the longer we stared at them, the less they seemed willing to move. Celie tried to follow my example, but she was only parroting my answers. Faced with a new problem, she looked dazed and bewildered all over again. It exhausted me.

One afternoon, her usual ride was canceled and I called Jon to tell him I would drive Celie home. I could hear a pan clattering in the background, and it was obvious he was in the midst of dinner preparations. He offered to come get her himself, he didn't want to impose, but I insisted. "It's no big deal," I said.

Celie followed me out of the building, watching the older students skipping on ahead, in twos and threes, laughing together, whacking each other with backpacks, calling names good-naturedly. I wondered if Celie had a group of friends at school, or if she floated around alone, a small island of unhappiness no one dared touch.

In my car, she curled up inside her jacket, though it wasn't very cold out, and stared out of the window. I turned the radio on low, a local pop station. "Do you like music?" I asked. A feeble attempt, I knew, but I thought any conversation might be better than none, and there had to be some way to get through to her. She shook her head, then shrugged.

"I like Judy Garland," she said. She seemed to suspect my silent re-action—*Judy Garland?*—and added, "I like old movies, especially musicals. Me and my dad watch them."

"I like old movies, too. What's your favorite?"

"Meet Me in St. Louis," she said. "And *Singing in the Rain,* and every Christmas we watch *Holiday Inn."*

"Do you like *The Wizard of Oz?"*

"It's okay, kinda long. But I like it when she sings 'Somewhere over the Rainbow.' It was my mom's favorite song. She always sang it to me when I was little." She paused, "We played it at her funeral."

I was stunned by this revelation, by the suddenly easy way she had of talking about her mother, the one subject I had thought taboo. Even though she had told me about the shoes on our first visit, I hadn't dared ask any more questions. For the first time it occurred to me that maybe she wanted to talk about her mother. I realized that, though my friends and colleagues frequently asked me how I was doing, thus hinting at my loss, none of them ever asked about or mentioned Dill. It seemed strange now, and I wondered why I hadn't noticed before. Dill was my husband for six years, the person I was with every day, talked to about everything, loved with all my heart. When he was gone, he had still stayed with me, every day, because I didn't forget. How could I? Yet my friends seemed to act as if he never existed. Celie, a mere child of ten, seemed to know deep down that the way to keep her mother with her was to talk about her, keep her in the forefront. When I came to a stop-light, I realized I was holding my breath.

"My husband, Dill," I said slowly as the light changed and I drove on, "he used to like old movies, too. We watched them almost every weekend. Sometimes he fell asleep halfway through, and he was always disappointed when he woke up. That's why we rented them on video, to watch our favorite parts over again."

"Yeah, we do that, too," Celie said, brightening a little.

"Dill always ate when we watched TV or movies—popcorn, Milk Duds, cornflakes, it didn't matter what. He just thought you should *really* enjoy yourself when you were watching something."

Celie smiled then, her dimples pressing into her cheeks. "My mom made this thing called nutty mix, it was just different cereals and chocolate chips. There were supposed to be nuts, but I don't like nuts so she left 'em out for me. So it was kinda funny that we called it nutty mix. My dad never makes it, though," she added somberly.

We were silent for a few minutes. Then I asked, "Does your dad talk about your mom very much?"

Celie looked out of her window again, and I wondered if she would answer. The nylon of her jacket swished softly as she moved in her seat. Finally, she said, "Sometimes he says he misses her, but he doesn't say a lot. He thinks it makes me too sad. But it doesn't. I don't want to forget her. That's what I'm afraid of. Sometimes I think I almost can't remember what she looked like, before she got sick and lost her hair and everything, so I look at this picture I have of her. She was really pretty."

We had stopped in front of her house. It was a ranch style, simple but elegant in a way, with a beautifully landscaped yard, a weeping cherry tree bowing over the front walk. I wondered if Celie's mother had planted the tree, knowing how it would bloom purple and lilac each spring.

"There's my dad," Celie said, opening her car door. Jon stood at the front door, holding a tea towel in one hand. He waved, and when I rolled down my window he shouted, "Thank you, Anna! I really appreciate it."

"No problem," I called back. "Bye, Celie," I said. She turned slightly and waved, then went inside. Jon stood a moment longer, in his stocking feet, as if considering coming out to the driveway to speak to me, but I started backing away, waving again, and he turned and went in after his daughter. After the door was closed, I stopped my car halfway down the block and looked back at their house. It was brightly lit, cheerful, the kind of house you would want to go inside and look around, stay awhile. I felt like the Little Match Girl, peering in the warmly lit windows of people's homes, guessing at their lives, their happiness. Even though I knew Jon and Celie weren't particularly happy, I thought, At least they're trying.

M artin rapped on my office door, and I looked up. "Come on in," I said, smiling. "How have you been? How's your little brother?"

"Fine," he said. "He's doing great. You'd never know anything happened to him, except he has a little trouble with math. Adding, subtracting. We have to work with him on it." He lingered in the doorway, as if not sure he wanted to come in. There was something else on his mind.

"Come on in," I said again. "I'm not that busy. What's up?"

Martin slouched into a chair. "Miss Rainey, I was wondering about something."

"Yes?"

"You and Jay."

"Jay?"

"You know, *Jesús*? Jay?" he said impatiently. "My next-door neighbor, Jay Hernandez, the guy you were going out with?"

I blushed deeply, taken aback. "We weren't really going out, you know. We just—" It was none of his business. I wasn't going to tell a sixteen-year-old about my sex life, such as it was. Horrified, I wondered if Jay had told him about our brief affair. "Why are you asking me about this?" I asked, bristling a little.

"He really liked you," Martin said simply. "I think he thought you liked him, too."

"I did. I do," I said. "But this is something between adults, between us. He shouldn't be talking about it to you."

"He isn't. I mean, I just can tell, because when I said something about you once, he got all weird. I know it ain't—isn't—my business, but I just thought, maybe you could give him another chance. He's a really nice guy, you know. He comes over to see James every day."

"I know he's a nice guy, Martin. He's a great guy. We're friends, that's all." Some friend I was, I thought. I would never see Jay again unless we bumped into each other on the street, and then he would probably turn and walk the other way.

"Is it because he's not white?" Martin asked.

I balked, confused. I pictured Jay, the caramel of his bare chest, the black licorice of his hair. I stared at Martin. "What are you talking about?"

He looked embarrassed. "You know—he's Latino."

"And? So?"

He shrugged.

"Don't you know me better than that?" I snapped.

"I'm sorry."

"He's just a lot younger than I am," I said, more calmly. "And sometimes people fit and sometimes they don't."

"Okay, I understand," Martin said meekly, standing up. I wondered if he was telling the truth, if Jay had talked about me and sent him to try to find out if I was receptive.

"Martin, please don't talk about this with anyone, okay? You have to respect my privacy. I lost my husband. I'm not really trying to date. And if Jay is wondering, well, you can tell him that."

Martin bowed his head a little. "He didn't ask me to ask you, if that's what you think. I just sort of wish you were together. It would be nice, that's all." I didn't know what else to say. I moved some paper clips around in a circle on my desk blotter. "Sorry I bothered you," Martin added, heading toward the door.

"You never bother me, Martin," I said.

When he was gone, I put my head down on my desk. It was so much easier when no one expected anything of me, when people left me alone, the lonely widow, walking around the electricity of my grief. Now it seemed everyone—Jon and Celie, Jay, Martin, the other students—wanted something. I could feel them all pulling me back into the real world, into life. I still didn't want to go, not completely. There were moments, though, when I tiptoed closer, against my better judgment. When Celie smiled at me, for instance, and when I saw Jon in the doorway in his socks, his shirttails pulled loose. I don't know what it was about that image that had struck me so, but I kept thinking about it, about him.

Mrs. VanderWal stood on the landing outside my door, smelling of meat loaf. I knew the source of the aroma because she had offered me some. She held it out on a platter, brown and moistly lumpy as dog food. I politely declined; I'd just eaten, I told her. "No offense, but I sort of need to know where we stand," she said.

"I think I'd like to stay on, if that's all right with you," I said. I handed her another month's rent.

"Great. I'm glad. Well, if you need anything at all, just come on down and knock. Mr. VanderWal and I are usually around, day or night. Since he retired, we don't seem to move much at all." She laughed a little. "Funny, we thought as soon as we didn't have to work so hard, we'd go do all the things we never had time for. Now all we have is time, and we sit around like bumps on a log."

"Well, if it makes you happy," I said.

Mrs. VanderWal looked puzzled for a moment, as if thinking over my casual remark. "I guess it does," she said finally, then waved and turned to head back down the stairs.

I remembered Dill joking about what we would be like as "old retired people." We would travel, of course—to Italy and Spain, spend a weekend in Paris in between. Maybe we would go skiing again, Dill said, though I laughed at that. The one time we had gone, with friends to Utah shortly after we were married, I had gotten the flu and skied only one time. I was a novice, and just the ride up on the ski lift had terrified me. Looking down the mountainside, the sheer whiteness I would have to maneuver made me nearly sick all over again. But I had done it, Dill patiently offering me tips, showing me how to lean into the slope, how to swing my body and arms around to make a turn, how to stop. Our friends at home had been impressed at my daring, since I never before had demonstrated any athletic prowess, besides hiking now and then. They all knew how I felt about swimming, and that I was a little afraid of heights, too.

But I had a photograph to prove it—on the top of one of the crests, a gangly young photographer had offered to immortalize us on skis. We leaned into each other, holding our poles to the sides, and grinned. The sky was bright blue, the sun blinding on the snow, so we kept our goggles on. When we received the photograph in the mail a few weeks later, we laughed because it looked fake, as if we had donned ski suits and boots, stood against a studio backdrop. The scenery was too perfect, we seemed so posed, smiling in the bright light, our hair unruffled by any wind. But it remained one of my favorite pictures of us, because we were on vacation, away from work and stress and household projects. We were in a resort town, eating big meals, and sleeping in a huge rough-hewn bed. When I was feeling better, we made love in front of the fireplace. Dill paused once to throw another log into the dying flames while I held my breath and quickly pulled him back to me. I was astounded to realize that I remembered it all—the scratchy blanket, the smell of smoke, the sharp edge of cold every time we moved away from the fire, the soft blond hairs on Dill's bare forearm, the pressure of his fingers on my skin—every detail.

I thought about Celie memorizing her mother, the things she did, how she sang, a day when they bought shoes.

I looked at my window, where the leaves pressing against the glass were beginning to dry out and redden. Seasons were changing, life was going forward, and I was inching onward, like it or not. What good did remembering do? The past simply continued to recede, further and further away, a dot on the horizon, then gone.

I went back to gathering the dishes I had used, wiping the countertop, setting the kettle on for tea. I sat down to wait for the whistle, turned on the TV, and found an old movie, starring, of all people, Judy Garland. One of the unhappiest people in Hollywood, I thought, as I watched her beam and sing, her wide-set eyes so bright with promise.

Curling my feet underneath me on the sofa, I said out loud, "I wonder if she drank. Her voice was always so husky." It was strange hearing my own voice in the room. It had been so long since I'd had a dinner companion, though, and I just felt like talking.

Then, just underneath my heartbeat, I heard Dill respond. He said, "You'd drink, too, if you'd had to run around a yellow brick road with adults in lion suits and coffeepots on their heads."

I laughed aloud, thinking that would be just the thing he would say, if he were there. Though, of course, he wasn't.

H ey, Miss Rainey," Sheena called out. "Guess what?"

"What?" I said. We were standing in the corridor between classrooms and offices, with minutes to spare before the tutoring sessions began. Girls were jockeying for position near one of the new college tutors, a sophomore named Jack, who was tall and gorgeous and smiled down upon all of them like a benign prince. I saw Sheena glance his way, too, before turning back to me.

"My mom is getting married," she said.

"Oh. Is that good? Are you glad?"

Sheena shrugged. "Yeah. For her. I mean, I like Lance and all, he's a good guy. He plays with my brothers and lets me use his car, stuff like that. So, I guess you could do worse for a stepdad." She was smiling, or trying to. I pulled her gently into my office and closed the door.

"Is there something else?" I asked. To my surprise, Sheena began weeping, but noiselessly, as if she thought it inappropriate. I put my arms around her and waited for her to explain, but she kept on crying. "What is it?" I said quietly, through her hair, which was pressed against my face.

She pulled away, sniffling. "It's like, now it's final. You know?"

"What is?"

"Like, my dad is gone and he's never coming back. I mean, I knew it; of course I know he's *dead*." She paused, wiping her eyes, which were red. "But when Lance was just this guy my mom dated, who stayed overnight sometimes, I still kind of thought it was temporary. That someday things would go back to normal." She looked to the side, her jaw tightening. "Isn't that stupid? God, I'm so stupid."

"No, you're not," I said. "It makes perfect sense." I understood, and it broke my heart. We were the same, this sixteen-year-old girl and I; we wanted our old lives back. I said, "I keep hoping for the impossible, too. And there's nothing wrong with it, as long as you *know* it's impossible, and you get on with your life in spite of it." It was good advice, I knew, though I wouldn't accept it myself. I was a fraud.

Sheena looked as though she had more she wanted to say, but she turned away, pulling her thoughts back into herself. I didn't try to stop her.

Suddenly I thought I owed her more, that I had to reach out further. "Come see me any time, okay?" I said at the doorway. She nodded, eyes still watering.

"Okay," she said.

"And bring me some salsa—you promised." I paused. "Hey, you're going to be *fine*," I said.

Finally she smiled, and then loped down the hallway to her tutoring room. I thought about how easy it was to placate a kid. You just listened for what she wanted to hear and then you said it, simply and earnestly. It was like dropping a rock into a little box and wrapping it all up, neat and pretty, handing it over: "Here." And if you were a good enough con artist, the recipient would think it the greatest thing she had ever seen. And it cost you nothing at all.

Celie came in dripping wet and not even bothering to wipe the rain from her hair or face. I led her to the rest room and handed her paper towels, one after another, until she dried herself off. "It must really be pouring out there," I said. I hadn't been out of my office all day, had eaten my lunch at my desk, trying to work on a grant proposal Jillian had asked me to write.

"Yeah," Celie said. "I was walking and it started raining harder. I didn't have an umbrella."

"What happened to your ride?" I asked. "I thought the McMillans drove you from school every day."

"I didn't want to ride with them," she said, scowling as she threw the paper towels in the trash can and walked out of the rest room.

When we were settled at my desk, I asked her, "Did something happen?"

Celie looked at me as if deciding whether or not to trust me. Then she said, "She thinks I'm fat because of my mom."

"What?"

"She says I use food as a substitute for my mom, and that it's normal but if I got some help I could learn to stop doing that. That's what she says."

"Who says?"

"Mrs. McMillan."

I sat back, aghast. "When did she say this?" I asked, as if it mattered in what context such conversation had arisen. I couldn't imagine what would provoke an adult to say such a thing to a child, especially one like Celie, who already struggled to make it through each day.

"I don't know, last week, I guess. She dropped off Margo at basketball practice and then she brought me home. So it was just me and her. And I said I was glad it was Thursday because my dad always makes pizza on Thursday nights, and then she said she was worried about me, and all that other stuff. It was weird, and it made me feel bad." She spoke matter-of-factly, as if in fact, it made her feel nothing, but it was obvious Celie had learned to shove her emotions someplace private when necessary. "I told her I didn't need a ride today, that I had a way to get here."

"That wasn't a nice thing for her to say," I said finally, thinking, *Bitch.* I wondered if Celie had told her father about it, and then I wondered if I should; I didn't know how much to get involved.

Celie seemed to want to change the subject, because she took out her homework and opened the math book. It was virtually the same assignment we had been working on to no avail for two weeks. I had run out of clever tactics for explaining long division. The numbers could be characters, animals, cakes, secret codes—it didn't matter. None of it made any sense to Celie. I dreaded going through it all over again. As I tried to think of a new angle for explaining the concepts, I wondered whether, if I told her how I had divided my own life into smaller and smaller compartments until there didn't seem to be much left, she would understand the metaphor. But of course, she was just a little girl.

Celie pushed her damp hair out of her face and sharpened a pencil with a little sharpener shaped like a dinosaur. Then she bent over the paper and wrote the first numbers.

I sighed softly so she could not hear me and then moved my chair around to her side of the desk. "Okay," I said gamely. "We have to divide eighty-four into thirteen hundred and forty-four. They're both even numbers, so it should come out even, right?"

"Okay," she said robotically. As if in a trance, she leaned over the desk and worked the problem. "It goes *into,*" she murmured, and I dared not interrupt and break the spell. I looked at the paper. She had done it, step by step. The answer, sixteen, perched atop the box like a trophy. She turned to me, smiling so hard her dimples were deep gashes in her cheeks.

"You did it," I said, astounded.

"I get it," she said in a dazed voice. Then, "Let's do another one," she said. She copied the next problem and the one after that. In thirty minutes she'd done fifteen more problems, scribbling along the margins when she needed to try out a solution. When she was finished it seemed nothing short of miraculous, no less amazing than James finally sitting up in his hospital bed.

I drove her home again, since her father was expecting Mrs. McMillan to drop Celie off after she picked up her own daughter from basketball practice. It was such a perfect arrangement, he probably thought, having no idea the woman was torturing Celie in the car with cruel comments and insensitive advice. I knew I had to tell him, but I hardly knew him. I wondered if I should call later, after Celie was in bed.

When we pulled into the driveway, however, Celie said, "Can you come in? I want to tell my dad what happened." I thought she had read my mind, but she added happily, "He won't believe it!" and I understood she was referring to the math, not Mrs. McMillan.

I followed her to the back door, rushing through the downpour, and Jon opened the door, clearly surprised to see me there.

"Celie has some news for you," I told him.

When she told him, Jon beamed, then lifted his daughter off the ground as if she were featherweight, and I was moved by the ease with which he did it—the fact that he showed her she was his little girl, no matter what anyone else saw or thought. I didn't want to spoil the event with unpleasant tidings, so I said I had to go.

"Great job, Celie," I said. "I'm really proud of you."

"Thanks," she said, suddenly shy.

"Hey, do you want to stay for dinner?" Jon asked, turning to me. I stopped at the door. I was inside the glowing house I had stared at the week before. I hesitated, then nodded.

"Okay," I said and stepped back across the threshold.

Jon had prepared a simple, slightly bland chicken in cream sauce, which seemed like something invented for children's palates. I ate it heartily, though, realizing I was very hungry. Celie fell silent again, as she had when we first met, though without the antagonism I'd sensed then. She seemed to have a lot on her mind and I thought it better to let her be, rather than try to force conversation. After she had finished eating, Celie politely excused herself, and Jon let her go. "Hey, good job," he said smiling. "I knew you could divide and conquer." Celie smiled and cleared her plate. She smiled at me, too, as she left the room.

"So, where do you do your work?" I asked Jon, feeling awkward when the two of us were alone.

"I have a small studio," he said, passing a bowl of white rice to me. "I do the usual, you know, weddings, family portraits, things like that."

"And senior pictures?" I asked, smiling, knowing how my students prepared for theirs months in advance, planning wardrobe changes and props to pose with.

Jon shook his head. "No, I have an assistant do those. It brings in a lot of our bread and butter, but I can't do them myself—all those kids want to look like movie stars, and I can't bear it."

"Oh," I said. "I think they just want to look glamorous—you know, grown-up."

"But they aren't grown-up," he argued calmly. "They're just kids. I can't make them look like something they aren't yet. It seems *false*."

I thought he was being too sensitive and judgmental; at the same time I saw his point. He pushed himself away from the table. "Let me show you something," he said. When he returned, he handed me two photographs. The first was of a ruddy, pleasant-looking young woman in a sweater seated against a tree trunk that was obviously made of painted Styrofoam. Paper leaves were scattered on the ground around her. Her face was smiling, though strangely flat, as if she were a mannequin. The second photograph was of the same woman, a little older, sitting in the real outdoors, the sky behind her pewter gray, her hair blowing, a strand of it stuck to her lip, though she kept smiling.

"See," Jon said, standing over me, pointing to the first picture. "That's my wife, Sandra, taken by an amateur, one of my competitors when I first opened my studio. It was right before we met. The other one I took a few years later." He cleared his throat. "I mean, I am not trying to brag, but you can see which photograph captures the real person, right?" His voice wavered a little, as if I might not.

"Yes," I said. "The truth is, I've always hated posed studio portraits."

"Me, too!" he said, then sighed. "It's hard. When I take a photograph of a bride and groom, or their parents, or whomever, I wait until I think I can see the real thing, relaxed, not the artifice. Then I take the picture. Most of the time, it works."

"It sounds like you have a real talent," I said.

Jon was silent. He had one more photograph in his hand, and he set it down on the table. It was of a woman sleeping. She was completely bald, and there were no eyelashes on her closed gray lids. She looked almost lizardy, her face translucently pale, with bluish veins visible in her temple. She appeared chiseled from marble.

"That's Sandra one day before she died," Jon said. "I wanted to remember her that way, too, because it was how she was for such a long time. But she was still beautiful, peaceful. Exactly like this."

I swallowed. For the first time I wished I had a photograph of Dill, just sleeping, on his last day. I'd had no idea, though, that it was the last day. I never dreamed that would be the end. Jon scooped up the photographs and tucked them into his shirt pocket.

"I have others," he said, and led the way from the kitchen to a paneled den, furnished with a faded sofa and easy chair, a television and a stack of children's videos. I looked around, expecting more photographs of Sandra, glowing as if with heavenly light, but instead the walls were covered with black-and-white photographs clearly taken during the Depression, and World War II. I recognized some of them though I couldn't name the artists. "Walker Evans," Jon said, pointing. "And that one is by Lee Miller. No Ansel Adams," he added, and laughed. "I'm not fond of nature pictures, just people. They're all reproductions, of course."

"I like them," I said. "You have a nice house."

"Sandra did most of the decorating, except for the photos."

"It's nice," I said again, feebly.

"Go ahead, sit down," he said then. I sat on a corner of the sofa. Jon sat down, too, on the edge of the coffee table facing me. His stance and earnestness made him seem like a gentle therapist, and I wondered if he were still attending the SOLO group, and if it had influenced his perspective. Ready to listen, watching for body language. All of a sudden, I wanted to tell him everything.

"How do you live here?" I blurted.

"What do you mean?"

"I mean, here, in her house, with all the things she picked out and used and sat in. Isn't it hard?"

Jon leaned forward just slightly, elbows on his knees. He seemed to be thinking it over, and I wondered if it had never even occurred to him to question it; where else would he live? In a dorm room?

"It's our home," he said quietly. "Celie was born here, it's all she's known for ten years. And, you know that her mother died here, too. Celie saw her at her worst, through chemo and all of that, so it wasn't as if she wasn't prepared for it. After the funeral, it took time, I admit, to feel *comfortable* without her here—" He paused, and I thought I saw him reconsidering his choice of words. Obviously, *comfortable* was a stretch.

"Anyway," he went on, "I think Celie actually needs signs of her mother around her. It wouldn't be right to clear it all away." I said nothing, just sat on the sofa and looked at my hands in my lap. Jon reached forward and touched my arm lightly. "I understand that it's different for you. You didn't have time to get used to the idea, did you?"

I shook my head. "No. I didn't. One minute he was there, then he was gone." He handed me a tissue and I blew my nose. Then I told him how it had happened, leaving nothing out, not even my ruthless criticism while I waited for the ambulance. I reiterated my deadly role. I told him about the list, and how I had failed to fix the garage door in time. I had never told our SOLO group the truth.

When I finished, Jon said, "I'm just wondering—why didn't Dill fix the garage door?" It was such a typical guy comment, I thought, expecting the man to do anything involving screws and wiring.

I shrugged, blew my nose again. "Oh, I took care of all the household stuff. Neither of us was handy, so I would call in the expert. But, of course, I didn't." I paused, not wanting to dwell on it anymore.

"Anyway, that's what happened. An aneurysm, and he was gone."

"Well, I'm sorry," Jon said, and I knew he meant it.

"I didn't mean to unload on you like this," I said apologetically, standing up. "Thank you for dinner." He stood, too, so that we were only a couple of feet apart.

"You're welcome. And thank you for all your work with Celie. It means a lot, this breakthrough."

I smiled and we stood there, me standing too close to the table, wedged between it and the sofa. I didn't know what to do or say, or if I should move, or wait until he spoke.

"Well," he said. "Take care, Anna."

As I neared the door of the den, I thought I felt a vibration, as if he were about to reach out an arm and stop me, and for a moment I felt certain he was going to step forward and kiss me, and I waited, debating in my head over whether or not I wanted him to. I walked slowly, to see if he would, wondering how I would react. I didn't have a chance to find out because he only stepped aside to let me pass.

I closed the back door behind me and walked to my car in the rain.

"Huh," I said aloud when I got behind the wheel. "That was weird."

"He doesn't want to make a move, you scared him away the first time," Dill said.

I whipped around to look at the empty seat beside me. "No, I didn't," I said. "He's just shy, and I don't blame him. It's horrible. No one should have to do it all over again—dating. Which is all your fault."

"Sorry," he said, though he sounded faintly mirthful. It was strange how easily I accepted the sound of his voice, not sure whether it was real or simply throbbing in my head. I may have been talking to myself, but I answered Dill as if he were sitting right there.

"Anyway, it wasn't a date, I don't know what I'm saying. We just had dinner. I'm helping his daughter. That's all."

"I know," he said, and then he didn't say anything else so I just drove home.

He wasn't really there, he couldn't have been, but when I crawled into bed, he was. I closed my eyes for only a moment, and then opened them. Dill was on his side, fully dressed, as if he had come home late and didn't have the energy to remove his clothes before falling into bed beside me. I kept looking at him, blinking and then looking harder. I didn't reach out to touch him, though. I thought that would spoil it all. Either he would feel so real it would devastate me—or he would disappear.

"Go to sleep," he said.

"I can't," I whispered.

"Why are you whispering?"

"I don't know." I paused, closed my eyes, and just listened for a moment to the silence, waiting for him to speak again. When he didn't, I said, "It's been so long."

"I know. I miss you, too, Annabelle," he said. No one had called me that in nearly a year, and no one ever had except Dill. I began to cry at the sound of it, but he laughed a little, saying, "I didn't mean to make you feel bad."

"You don't," I said, with my eyes still closed. "You never made me feel bad, ever. Except when you left." I needed him to hear the truth, to know how much he had hurt me, how hard it was alone, and I wanted him to explain exactly what had happened. There had to be an explanation. All along I had thought it was too absurd to be believed. "I'm just so tired of it all," I said.

"I know. Go to sleep now."

"That's not what I meant," I said. I opened my eyes, and he was gone. I knew I had probably been asleep all along, and woken from a dream. Still, I sat up in my bed and ran my hand over the other side. I leaned over and sniffed the pillow, then switched on the lamp to look for signs. A small impression in the mattress, a stray hair, anything. But there was nothing. Nothing at all. And for the thousandth time I was dumbfounded by how heavy nothing could feel.

I bought groceries, I folded my laundry, I remembered to pay my bills, to trim my hair, to file my nails. I cleaned the toilet, put fresh Contac paper on the bathroom shelves, and took walks after work for exercise, to clear my head. I browsed the magazine racks at the supermarket and bought trashy stories about Hollywood stars and their tumultuous lives. I talked to Lydia and Lexi and my mother on the phone. I chatted with Mrs. VanderWal about the weather and ran into the elusive Mr. VanderWal in the driveway, where he was scrubbing the tires of his Lincoln with a nail brush. I counseled Martin about his need to work harder in his chemistry class, even if it seemed utterly pointless. I paid extra attention to Sheena, who moped through the halls. I handed Jillian monthly progress reports, neatly typed, and shared chocolates with Natalie at her desk. People who knew me smiled; I knew they were thinking, She's doing all right. I could feel them sighing with relief. What they didn't know, however, was my amazing secret. For months I had grieved over Dill's absence; now he seemed to be everywhere. I heard him speaking to me, softly, matter-of-factly. Perhaps he had been there all along and I'd just failed to see him through my fog. Sometimes we talked, and sometimes we didn't. But it wasn't like living with a ghost. It was as if I were living with a fragment, a piece of my very self that had broken off, like a missing limb. I could feel it, even as I knew it was gone and I kept reaching for it.

Martin was sitting on the top step outside the Upward Bound offices when I returned one afternoon after a meeting. He wore headphones, bobbing slightly with the music, and his eyes had an intensely faraway look in them. I thought he didn't see me approaching, but as soon as I neared the steps, he whipped off the headphones and looked down at me.

"Hey, Miss Rainey," he said, suddenly serious.

"Hey, Martin. How're you doing?" I started up the stairs, shouldering my bag.

"Fine," he said, but his tone held me there. I waited, and he said gravely, not meeting my eyes, "I hate to tell you, but he's moved on. He's gone."

I stood perfectly still, allowing his words to sink in. How could he know? I wondered, my heart thumping. I could feel myself flush, too, and struggled to recover. "I—" I started to say, to defend myself, but I wasn't sure what words would make sense.

"I just thought you should know, you know, in case you were having second thoughts. I didn't want you to call him and be, like, embarrassed."

I was confused, but then it began to come clear. He was talking about *Jay*. He's "gone" meant "in love;" I remembered Martin once informing me. "Oh," I said. "That's thoughtful of you, Martin. I appreciate it." I sat down on the step beside him.

Martin shrugged. "Well, I just thought—" he began again, looking pained.

"It's okay," I said. "What's her name?" I asked, to feign interest. I was immensely relieved, in more ways than one.

"Zoe, I don't know her last name. I think she's his friend's cousin or something like that. They met at a wedding."

"Well, that's good," I said, smiling.

"It is?"

"Yes, I'm really glad for him. He's a great guy."

"So, you're not jealous?" Martin asked.

I shook my head. I thought about how the kids always got involved in each other's love lives, and it was amusing, in a way, that Martin cared so much about my happiness. "What about you?" I said then, teasing. "Who's your main squeeze these days?"

Martin laughed, fidgeted with his headphones in his hands. "No one right now. Or at least, no *one,* if you know what I mean."

"You really are a Romeo, aren't you," I said.

"I try, Miss Rainey. You always tell me to try, right?"

We both laughed. I looked at Martin, growing into a lean and solid young man, his eyes bright, his smile wide and quick. It was like looking at my own child, so close to me but so near slipping away, growing up and disappearing into the masses. I felt a pang at the imminent loss, even though Martin still had two more years till graduation. I thought, That's what life is all about, really. One loss after another. You just had to get used to it.

Celie continued to come every Tuesday and Thursday, sometimes to work at math, though with less struggle, other times to review spelling words or rewrite a book report. Her grammar was weak, and she was lazy correcting it. I wondered if she just wasn't very ambitious, and thought perhaps there was nothing wrong with it, with just being mediocre. However, I knew her ongoing indifference—except for our one success with division—had nothing to do with school.

I thought I could help her. Or, maybe, I thought we could help each other. One day, when she looked up from her social studies book and asked me what "branches of government" meant, I didn't answer right away. She was used to this by now; she understood the classic tutoring tactic of forcing the student to think harder, dig deeper. She was used to me waiting, and she often sighed, or scowled, or groaned and leaned back in her chair. Often she said, "This is so dumb," and I wasn't sure if she meant the homework or our time together. Even so, she had continued to warm to me, a little, and I knew that she respected me if for no other reason than that I was suffering as she was.

"Celie," I said. "Do you ever talk to your mom?" She looked startled. She was waiting to hear an explanation for separation of powers, and I knew this came out of the blue. She stared at a spot just over my head, so I added, "I mean, do you tell her things, privately?"

Celie regarded me suspiciously, as if it were a trap, then she shrugged and said, "Sometimes. Yeah."

I took a breath, and a big chance, and asked, "Does she ever answer?" The question hovered over us then, and Celie looked down at her hands, perhaps at her shoes, the ones that were too tight though she continued to wear them, rain or shine. She was swinging her feet underneath her chair, and then she looked at me. "My mom doesn't talk to me. She's dead."

"I didn't mean to upset you, I swear," I said. "I just wondered if you could feel her presence. When someone dies, they're gone, but part of them, their spirit, lives on I believe. And maybe it's just my imagination, but sometimes lately I feel Dill's spirit. That's all."

I had thought I could comfort Celie by letting her talk about her mother, but selfishly, I wanted her to reassure me that it was normal and sane to live the way I was living. But Celie was a child, and I had pushed her too far. She didn't hear her mother's voice, and I could tell from her crestfallen expression, she would have given anything for it.

"I sort of feel her," Celie said slowly, as if she were trying to convince herself, or perhaps she just thought she hadn't given the right answer the first time. "When I'm falling asleep. My dad always tells me to remember to say my prayers, and I do, but I forget I'm praying to God and I sort of pray to my mom." She glanced at me. "Do you think that's bad?"

I shook my head. "No, I think it's perfectly fine. I'm sure God understands. He knows your mother watches over you." It sounded trite, the kind of thing people say to children to make them feel better— give them guardian angels and tooth fairies and Santa, and they won't have to worry about death and disaster.

We went on with the lesson. I had her read aloud from her book, and then I drew a tree with three sturdy, equal branches and labeled them executive, legislative, judicial. I had her draw what she thought symbolized each, and she surprised me, taking her time to make an accurate likeness of the president perched on his branch, and judges in black robes like nuns. When she got to Congress, she stopped and asked me again how many representatives and senators there were and I told her. I said that she didn't have to draw them all. She looked relieved, though

I believe she would have done it, taken more paper out and drawn five hundred and thirty-five people—anything to keep her mind off her mother's spirit. I should have told her that I had just been kidding, that it was all a dream and I never saw or heard Dill, but it was too late. The damage had been done.

My mother asked me if I wanted to meet her for lunch. It was an unusual invitation because it seemed she rarely went anywhere. I always went to see her at her house, where we would sit and talk and drink coffee until a sufficient amount of time had passed and I felt it was time to leave. But now she wanted to go out for Mexican food, in the middle of the day.

"There's new place, on Seventh Street," she said on the phone. "It's called Mama's Casa, I think. Isn't that cute? Like that woman in the Mamas and the Papas. Why don't we meet there?"

"That was Mama Cass, Mom," I said.

"What?"

"*Casa* means 'house' in Spanish. It's something else entirely."

"I don't know what you're talking about," my mother said.

"Never mind."

The restaurant was bright pink, the walls throbbing with color. I had to look away, down at my menu, to give my eyes a rest. The waitress brought giant bowls of tortilla chips, dark brown from frying, along with minced homemade salsa. I tasted it and understood what Sheena had been talking about. My mother was eating with gusto, chip after chip. She ordered a margarita, though I'd only ever seen her drink at holidays, and never in the daytime.

"Wow," I said. "It's kind of early for tequila, isn't it?"

My mother laughed. "Well, it's five o'clock somewhere in the world." I didn't know who this new woman was, this impostor pretending to be my mother. She told me, "They have the best vegetarian burrito here, you have to try it."

"You've been here before?" I asked. I didn't know my mother ever went out to eat, or that she liked vegetarian food. Maybe I didn't give her enough credit. Maybe she did have a whole other life I knew nothing about. Clubs and friends, maybe even men. The latter idea nearly floored me, and I was about to inquire when my mother said, "So are you seeing anyone?"

"Like who?"

"I don't know. I just wondered if you were—circulating at all."

"Circulating?" I was stunned. "Mom, I don't even think about that. I just can't." It was a lie, and I knew it.

"Anna," my mother said, and she looked me in the eye. It was as if she were finally really seeing me, and she had something to say. I could tell by her expression, the set of her lips, that it wasn't going to be small talk. "I haven't said anything before because I know it takes time to get used to this. Lord knows it took me years. And it's still hard sometimes. But you have to get on with your life, you know. You're still young." She paused. "Dill would want you to, too."

At the mention of his name, I flushed. She had said it, she acknowledged him. I glanced at the seat beside me to see if maybe he had heard and rushed right over. "Mom," I started. I didn't know what to tell her. How could I explain how it was? Now that I finally was considering trying to get on with my life, Dill had returned. How could I "circulate" now?

"You feel like you'd be betraying him," my mother said, as if she suddenly had Lydia's psychic powers. "But he is gone, sweetie, and it's okay to start to look around, to think about seeing other men."

"It sounds so crass," I blurted. " 'Other men.' Do you see other men?"

My mother smiled, infinitely patient. "Sometimes. No one regularly until recently. There's a man from church, Bill, I see about once a week. We have dinner or see a movie. He took me here," she said, waving an arm toward the restaurant. "It's a little more romantic at night because they use candles. It isn't so bright then." She turned up her nose at the noxious paint color.

"So," I said. "You have a boyfriend. I had no idea."

"Well, I wouldn't call him that. We're both sixty-something. He's just a 'special friend.' " The way she smiled and blushed horrified me. I didn't want to know any more, especially not what made Bill 'special.' I shook my head, laughed. But my mother-in-disguise wasn't going to let it go. "You should get out more, Anna. Meet people."

"I do meet people, Mom."

"You know," said my mother, ignoring me, "when your father died, he was fifty-four years old. Much too young to go, everyone said. Yet, it was his time. We don't know when our time will come, but everyone has to depart the station sooner or later. You just don't know what your ticket says until it's handed to you." I feared she was going to carry on with the train metaphor and I almost interrupted, but then she went on, "Some people say that since you could go at any time, you should treat every day as if it were your last. Well, that is just a lot of bunk, because if you did that, you'd be weeping all the time, saying good-bye to the same people you said good-bye to yesterday. You have to live your life! You can't sit around like a visitor. You *live* here." The food came then, and we busied ourselves with messy buritos. I was left wondering whom she was admonishing, herself or me.

It would just be dinner, a way to reciprocate. Surely he knew baby-sitters he could hire for one evening, and I could cook something from scratch in my new kitchen. I had apples for a pie; I could probably figure out how to assemble one. All I had to do was to call and ask him to come.

The girl who answered the phone wasn't Celie but, in fact, a baby-sitter named Cathy, who told me "Mr. Gordon" was out for the evening and could she take a message?

Out? I thought. Where would he go? It wasn't Tuesday, so it wasn't SOLO night—

"So, do you want to leave your name, or what?"

"Oh," I said, "Never mind. I'll call back later."

"He won't be home till late, like eleven-thirty, I think."

When I hung up, I continued to contemplate all the places Jon Gordon might be on a Wednesday night. A business meeting? He was a photographer, so it wasn't likely. Maybe he had an appointment, a special sitting for some clients, but why so late? Or maybe he played poker with a regular group of guys, a night of freedom from single parenthood when he could drink dark lagers and smoke cigars and even swear. Jon was growing more fascinating all the time, and the more I thought about his hypothetical comings and goings, the more I wanted him at my table, eating my pasta, talking without worry of Celie overhearing. I would pour more wine, I would let him have a cigar if he wanted; I could open the kitchen window and watch the smoke curl away. I had never kissed a man who smoked. It sounded rather earthy, sexy.

I thought of the list I had composed as a dreamy teenager, of all the traits I wanted in a man someday. I'd written it down in my careful longhand on a page of my diary:

Good looks—goes without saying, though I am not that picky. No nose hairs, though, and preferably no horn-rimmed glasses. Wire rims okay.

Sense of humor—not falling-down funny, but good-natured, able to joke and not take himself too seriously. No racist or sexist jokes. No blonde jokes; they are just stupid.

Tall? Not too. Just not shorter than me.

Smart—I couldn't bear it if I found out he had never heard of Tibet, like Jason, who thought it was a kind of hat, or like Alex in English, who always says "him and me." Picky, I know, but it's my life.

I laughed, thinking about my naïveté, and then sobered, thinking how perfectly Dill had fit every single requirement on my list. And then some. Once, I had even shown him the list, which I'd saved.

He skimmed it, looking serious, then said, "I could read this better with my horn rims. Have you seen them? Oh, and I can't find my nose-hair trimmer, either—"

"Stop it!" I said, laughing.

He went on, deadpan, "You know, a funny thing happened today. There were these two blondes, and one of them said she was going to Tibet, and I'm like, 'What's that?' and she's like, I don't know but him and me are going."

I couldn't imagine Jon Gordon, Jr., telling a joke of any kind, but then, I didn't know him that well yet. And I hadn't exactly put him in a ribald mood when I was at his house, talking about death. Maybe it was time to make a new list, or to forget about such lists altogether. Of course, Jon Gordon wasn't perfect, but he was here, in the flesh. And in my life as it was, that counted for a lot.

I drove Celie home the next evening, our regular routine now, Mrs. McMillan having been politely dismissed. I planned to ask her father out to dinner when we had a moment alone.

Celie fiddled with the automatic window, watching it glide up and down, halfway up, then halfway down again. Finally, she closed it and said, "I've been thinking about what you said."

"About what?"

"About my mom's spirit."

"Oh—listen," I said quickly, ready to douse the flames. "I don't think I should have brought that up like that, given you the idea that it was normal—"

"But you were right," she said, her eyes round. "My mom is there, I can feel her. I can even hear her voice."

I had to pull to the side of the road; I was too distracted all of a sudden to drive. My heart rose to a spot just below my larynx and I swallowed hard. I felt as if I had been preaching without a license on a street corner, steering the innocent to a truth based on no existing theology, on nothing more than wishful thinking.

"Celie," I said softly. "You don't have to try to convince yourself that you hear her. I know you are a smart kid, a wise one, in fact, and you have been handling your mother's death with more grace than any adult I have ever met. Certainly better than I have been handling my own loss." I stopped because she was looking away from me, her body rigid. "I really am sorry, Celie," I said. "I had no right to make you think—to give you false hope. I was only telling you what I felt, and really, what I felt was probably all my own imagination."

"It isn't imagination!" she shouted at me. Her voice was loud in the closed car, and she began pounding on the door, a small tantrum, an explosion of emotion she had been holding in for who knew how long. "My mom isn't gone. Not completely. I *know* she's there with me. She is!"

I didn't know what else to do but to let her rant, and to put the car into gear and slowly drive the rest of the way to her house, cautious around curves, coming to complete stops at yield signs, as if I were carrying a fragile load. In fact, I was.

When we got to the driveway, she was no longer talking. She had grown stonily silent, shutting out my attempts at peacemaking. I knew I had to walk her into the house and explain to her father what was wrong, and that it was all my fault. Just when I had thought I was helping Celie to navigate the dark waters of sorrow, instead I had been holding her head under, suffocating her.

"I'll go in with you, okay?"

"No," she said, opening her door.

"Celie, I want to explain—"

She stopped halfway out of the car and said, without looking at me, "Don't tell my dad about it. I will." She slammed the door and stomped to her house. I could see the back door light flick on and Jon coming out to meet her. Apparently, her expression had changed, because he didn't seem to think anything was amiss; he waved to me and closed the door.

I sat in the driveway for a long moment, debating with myself, then got out and impulsively knocked on the front door. When Jon opened it, I blurted, "We need to talk."

"What's the matter?" he asked, coming outside and closing the door behind him.

"I have something to confess," I said. "I think I may have given Celie the impression that she can talk to her mother, that she's still around."

"What do you mean?" Jon looked at me with alarm, as if he had sudden images of séances and tarot cards, my desk covered with candles when we were supposed to be working on multiplication.

"I just mean, I told her that sometimes I talk to Dill, and that it's comforting to feel him nearby. I thought it would help her, but I think she may have taken me too literally." I didn't think it would help to tell him that I did speak to Dill, literally.

"Well," Jon said, clearing his throat. He wrapped his arms around himself, rocked on his feet on the porch step. I looked down and saw that his socks had red stitching along the toe line. "Well," he repeated. "I guess that explains why she has been a little withdrawn lately, spending more time in her room. This isn't a good thing, Anna, I have to tell you. I know you didn't mean any harm, but I thought we were making progress. I've tried hard to let Celie grieve, but also to help her move on. I don't want her to be defined by this all the time—'the girl whose mother died.' It isn't healthy."

"I know. I'm so sorry," I said. Out of the corner of my eye I could see a small round face at the front window, framed by curtains. Celie was watching us, watching me. Her expression implored again, *Don't tell him*. And I realized that the reason she had wanted to keep it from him was so that she could continue to hold on to the belief. Now that Jon knew, he would try to reason with her, to talk her out of it, to uncurl her grip as if she were holding the crazy notion like a stolen coin in her fist. Now I felt even worse.

"Maybe I should talk to Celie," I said, a little desperately.

"I think I should talk to her," Jon said. He turned to go back inside. "And I think, if you don't mind, Anna, that you should stick to just tutoring as far as Celie is concerned."

After he left me standing there in the dark, I knew that any chance of dinner had evaporated, curling away like the imaginary smoke from his cigar. I thought of all the things I had done wrong in my life, large and small, and that it seemed some days I simply accumulated disaster, a magnet for bad ideas and poor judgment. Most of it I could do nothing about, but I knew that, somehow, I had to make it up to Celie.

To my surprise and relief, she appeared the following Tuesday, only a few minutes late. I had sat watching the clock, my stomach fluttering. I distracted myself by greeting the Upward Bound students when they came in before dispersing to their classrooms; I drank stale coffee; I listened to Natalie retell the entire plot from a mystery novel she had just finished reading; and I rearranged color-coded files. When Celie finally walked in, I braced myself for a tirade of accusations. Instead, she smiled her usual half smile, and sat down opposite my desk. Her hair was shiny and combed smooth across her scalp, then wound into two braids stiff as batons on the sides of her head. She saw me looking at them and said, "I did it myself, without even looking in the mirror. My dad doesn't know how to do hair."

"It's cute," I said.

"Thanks."

"Celie, are you doing all right?" I asked. She shrugged, and I wondered if I should press the point or obey her father's request that I stick to schoolwork. In other words, mind my own business.

"I don't have any homework," she said, taking off her backpack. "I didn't know if I even should've come today."

"I'm glad you did," I said.

"So, what are we going to do?"

"I guess we could review some math, if you want, or work on vocabulary for your test next week." When she turned up her nose at both suggestions, I paused, struck by an impulsive idea. "Or we could go ice skating."

"Now?"

"Sure, why not? I can leave a little early. We could stop at your house and get your skates."

She seemed to be thinking this over. "I keep them in a locker at the rink."

"Even better," I said.

On the drive there, Celie asked me if I knew how to ice-skate. I said that I didn't, but I was willing to try. "Maybe you can give me some pointers," I said. She nodded.

When we got to the main doors, we were stopped by a sign posting that the rink was closing early for reicing. We had ten minutes; skaters and parents were already exiting, brushing past us.

"Oh darn it," Celie said. "I forgot they do this on Tuesdays. They smooth it over every night, but on Tuesdays there are hockey games and they add more water and it takes longer." Now that I had come this far with her, offered her an excuse to forget her work, to do what she loved to do—and perhaps to forgive me in the bargain—I did not want to be dissuaded.

"Let me see what I can do," I said, and pushed my way through the glass doors.

The wiry boy at the ticket window appeared to be no more than sixteen, but he was prepared with the sorry-we're-closing speech; I could see his brows knit, his wide mouth working. I stopped him before he could say anything.

"Listen," I said in an urgent whisper. "You're in charge here, right?" I suspected that even the implication might be enough to make him amenable. He looked around as if someone might question the idea, and I took the opportunity to proceed. "I was wondering if you might be able to keep the rink open for just another, say, thirty or forty minutes?"

"Lady, I'm not supposed to let anyone in here after five o'clock. It's Zamboni time."

"But it's not five yet," I argued calmly. I looked behind me and saw that the rink was empty now. "Don't you think they could wait just a little longer to start on the ice?" I pushed one ten- and two twenty-dollar bills across the counter, underneath the glass shield. He looked at them, then at me.

The boy looked at the money again, probably as much as he earned in a week of this after-school job. "Okay, I'll go talk to Fred," he said.

"Fred," I said to Celie after the boy had disappeared from his post. "Fred is going to make it all right." Celie was trying hard not to laugh, and at the same time her brows were raised in astonishment that I had brashly confronted and bribed authority, such as it was, in order to get my way. And while I was sure I was furthering my position as a bad role model in her father's eyes, I felt my motives were laudable.

Five minutes later, as the doors were locked to the rest of the outside world, Celie and I were lacing skates and stepping onto the vast oval of ice. The boy at the desk had graciously gone behind the rental counter himself and handed me a size eight pair of white boots with gleaming silver blades. They looked as if they had never been worn. "You ladies have fun," he said suavely, winking at me. "You got till six."

I kept my jacket on, but Celie left hers on a bench, wearing her jeans and a green sweater. Already she was relaxed, waving her arms around in a warm-up, checking her laces.

"Ready?" she asked. I nodded and followed.

Clunky and inept, I clicked across the ice, while Celie glided and floated. I watched her for a moment, swaying atop my laden feet and trying not to fall just standing still. It looked so simple. I bent my knees a little and tried to force the blades to pull me along. Immediately my palms were flat on the cold surface. The ice was covered in white shavings from hours of skating, and I scooped up enough in one hand to make a Sno-kone. I hadn't skated since I was about eight years old, in Kara's backyard on a homemade rink that was bumpy and uneven. I had worn her brother's oversize skates, which twisted my ankles until finally I took them off and slid around in my fleece-lined boots. I remembered the liberating feeling, though, of slipping around in the cold air with Kara, laughing just to see our puffs of breath, staring up at the blank charcoal sky and then down at the black glass below us. This was different, the lights too bright, the sky a web of enormous metal beams. But Celie seemed enormously happy, skimming and twirling alone in the center of the bluey-white rink. Tiny shards of ice sprayed from her blades when she turned or stopped quickly, and her body seemed something else entirely—she was no longer chubby and clodding but moved with the lightness and grace of an Olympic skater twice her age and half her size.

After a few minutes, she raced over to where I was scissoring my feet back and forth in a futile effort at motion and stopped with an elegant swoosh. "Do you want some help?" she asked, slightly breathless. "Sure," I said. Celie took my hand and showed me how she bent just slightly, her back still straight, and how she pushed outward, her foot aiming in the direction she wanted to go.

"You make it look so easy," I said.

"It just takes practice, like anything," the wise child said. And she pulled me along as if I were a stubborn mule and my arm a tether.

When she let go, I was gliding, slowly, and I whooped with delight. "Hey, I'm skating!" I shouted to Celie, who had already turned into a mere flash of green across the rink, her braids flicking up like antennae.

"I knew you could do it!" she shouted back. And the way she smiled at me, I knew everything was fine.

"Ten more minutes, ladies," our teenage host called out from the bleachers. He paused for a moment to watch me and gave me an encouraging thumbs-up sign. I waved at him and glided, trying to catch up with Celie, which was impossible, but I was happy just trying. I was happy, period, inside a crystallized moment, for once not dwelling backward or worrying myself forward.

You should have seen her," I said in bed that night. "She is so—I don't know, complicated and endearingly simple at the same time."

"Like me?" Dill asked.

I laughed. "Yes, you always were simple."

"What about him?" he asked.

"You mean Jon?" I turned over onto my side as if he were lying on the other half of the bed and I couldn't bear to face him. "There isn't anything going on. I mean, I admit I thought we were becoming friends, going through the same thing more or less, but now I don't know if he even likes me. He's very protective of Celie, and he thinks I'm—subversive."

Dill laughed. "I doubt that."

I turned over and lay on my back, addressing the ceiling. "You should have seen the look on his face when I dropped off Celie, an hour late, our faces flushed; you would have thought I'd taken her out drinking at a bar."

Jon had tried to smile when I stated my case—Celie had no homework; I thought it would be good to get out of the academic atmosphere for a change and do what she liked; she taught me to skate—but I could tell he was dismayed. "Well, dinner's ready," he said to Celie, pointedly not looking at me or inviting me inside this time.

"Thanks," Celie said to me, grinning. "That was really fun."

"You're welcome," I said, not daring to add that we could do it again sometime. I wanted to tell Jon that not once had we mentioned Celie's mother, or my husband, had not even thought of death or loss or anything unpleasant for over an hour. We were free, I wanted to say, and it was wonderful.

"Well, thank you for bringing her home," Jon said curtly, as if there were any doubt that I would have.

"I'm sorry for any misunderstanding," I said. "We just had a little outing, and it was a lot of fun."

"I know. I just want to stick to some routine, some guidelines, that's all." He looked so pained when he said it, as if he didn't even agree with himself.

"Okay," I said, a little more defiant. "But I don't think an hour of skating did her any harm at all, even if it was out of her usual routine. Sometimes you have to color outside the lines a little—don't you know that?" He studied me for a moment as if he were going to argue or offer another reprimand, but he set his mouth in an unconvincing smile and told me good night.

"I don't know why I ever bothered with him," I told Dill.

"Because you think he looks like me," he said. I breathed in sharply. Jon was nothing like Dill, I thought. Yet, as I thought of him, my beloved apparition, I saw that maybe he was partially right. Jon was fair, pale and blond, with a faint fragility about him, even as he was tall and solid. You wanted to hold him and take care of him.

"The thing is," Dill was saying softly, "he has no sense of humor. Not a shred. And that is why it would never work."

And having said his piece, he was gone.

The point was moot, after all. Apparently the reason Jon hadn't made any overtures toward me the night I'd had dinner with him, though all along I had imagined I felt a humming attraction from him, was not that I had scared him away but that he had a girl-friend. Her name was Elizabeth, and he had been seeing her on Wednesday nights for several months and sometimes on Fridays if Celie slept at her friend Martha's house. Elizabeth was willowy and young, a mere twenty-six years old (though, after Jay, I could scarcely judge), and a sometime model for local department stores. Jon had photographed her when a new mall opened up and she was helping to advertise twin sets and leather pants.

I learned all of this from Celie, who pieced it together for me in sketchy vignettes the way children do, telling you one thing then something else seemingly irrelevant so that you have to play detective and find the connection. For instance, she told me that her father had invited "someone" over for Sunday dinner, then showed me pictures from the newspaper in which a model grinned at the camera with her lean, leathery thighs crossed at the ankles as she perched on a (fake, I thought) park bench.

"Here's another one," Celie said, turning the page to show me a more demure version, in ponytail and cashmere. Once I understood that the model was "someone," what struck me about the photos, aside from the fact that they belied Jon's apparent talent for capturing the natural and authentic, was that Elizabeth looked nothing like Sandra. She looked bold and sexy and decidedly unsaintlike. I wondered how Celie had found out about the Wednesday nights and occasional Friday nights (sleepovers for Elizabeth, probably), but I didn't dare ask. Celie was being as forthright as she knew how and telling me all she could or wanted to—the gist of it being that her father had a girlfriend and Celie was adjusting to it, in her own stoical way.

"Do you like her?" I gingerly asked Celie. Typically, she shrugged. "She's—pretty," I said then, trying to find something positive to say about the pictures.

"Yeah, she's nice, I guess," Celie said, folding up the newspaper advertisement as if it were Exhibit A and she needed to return it to the files. "But she's not like you," she added.

I smiled at the compliment and then thought, Maybe it wasn't really a compliment after all. Of course Jon would choose someone not like me—someone young and vibrant and happy, not someone burdened with sorrow like a heap of unwashed laundry that continued to grow higher all the time. If we had gotten together, our combined grief would have been a vast mound neither of us would have been able to stumble around after a while. In a way, I didn't really care; I realized that my vague interest in Jon had been based on nothing more than the fact that he knew what I was going through and that he had been a husband—one who did slightly resemble my own. He wasn't even my type, if there was such a thing. But Dill wasn't completely right. I had to believe that anyone who would date a girl whose nickname, Celie informed me, was Zipper had to have a sense of humor.

It was Jillian who noticed. I was passing through the hallway between the main office and one of the classrooms before tutoring sessions began, when she stopped me with a long-fingered grip on my arm.

"Anna," she said, the way a boss does before she tells you that you've been slacking off, or turning up late, or forgetting to hand in your reports on time. But what Jillian had on her mind was of a more personal nature. "You look terrible," she said.

"Oh," I said, automatically putting a hand to my hair, then glancing down at my skirt to see if it might be on backward. I was forgetting little things lately, I knew, and I supposed it was entirely possible I might not be groomed properly.

"It's your eyes," Jillian said softly, kindly. "You look like you haven't slept in days. Is that true? Are you holding up all right?"

It was enough out of the ordinary for Jillian to comment on an aspect of an employee's nonprofessional life; to have her so specifically scrutinizing caught me off guard. Also, she still had her hand on my arm, as if I were something wild that might try to get away. After a moment she let go but remained gazing at me with consternation.

"I guess I haven't been sleeping too well," I admitted. "I have a lot on my mind and I've been really busy . . ." My voice trailed off as I tried to recall what I had been doing during the wee hours. I'd made it sound like I was feverishly painting cabinets or scraping wallpaper. In fact, I did nothing. I wandered aimlessly around the three rooms of my rented home and circled from the kitchen, after a drink of water or wine, back to the sofa, where I curled up with an unread book and a blanket dragged from my bed as if I were a sleepy toddler. I wasn't sleepy at all, though; that was the problem. I couldn't remember the last night I had slept all the way till morning. Ever since Dill had shown up, it seemed I couldn't fall asleep anymore. I don't know if it was because I was desperate to have the time with him and feared he would leave if I didn't keep watch or if I simply had slipped into another kind of physical dimension, where sleep was unnecessary. I decided it wouldn't do to try to explain to Jillian the source of my insomnia, so I just shrugged and told her I was going through a phase and would probably snap out of it soon.

"Don't worry," I assured her. "I'm fine."

Jillian didn't appear convinced. "Why don't you take some time off, get some rest? Go to a movie or something, you know, just to have a break in your routine. Okay?"

I knew that Jillian's version of "okay" was rhetorical; what it meant was "Just do it." So I nodded and picked up my coat and bag and left.

I didn't head to the cinema, though, nor did I go home to sleep. I just drove around for an hour, turning down one side street after another, until I finally turned away from town and headed to the countryside. There were farms just five miles outside the city limits, and it was soothing driving along cornfields and apple orchards. It was autumn, and the fruit was heavy, tipping the branches down to arms' reach. As I drove, I listened to the radio, to popular stations playing love songs I didn't know so I couldn't sing along with them.

I thought about Jon, bent over the stove fixing dinner for his bright-eyed Zipper and, after Celie was asleep upstairs, drawing his lover into the den crowded with photographs. They would pull open the sofa bed and make love soundlessly, and Jon would forget all about the wife who had lounged there during her last days. He would be wrapped around the flesh-and-blood woman in his arms, her smells and skin and hair and fingers. And suddenly I knew that I wasn't jealous of her at all. I didn't want to be there with Jon, alone, making love on his sofa or anywhere else. If the opportunity had arisen, I think I would have panicked and fled. I wasn't ready for that kind of intimacy, in spite of my earlier, fleeting relationship with Jay. We had been two bodies, that was all. And I knew that I couldn't do now what I had done then, in the dorm room out of sheer desperation. I wasn't desperate anymore. And besides, I had Dill with me, watching over me, and though it didn't exactly offer consolation or even comfort, I had to hold on to whatever I could.

There was a tornado warning one night. I listened to the weather reports on the radio while I heated soup on the stove. The windows rattled as if demanding to be opened, and I obliged. I liked to hear storms, the threat of disaster hinted in the sound of wind and thunder. The air was alternately still and heavy, and then whipped into a frenzied breeze, branches outside the glass bending in self-protection. Clouds roiled, and the sky had the telltale yellowish tint that was rare and eerie, as in science fiction.

I didn't hope for disaster, but I liked the drama. I remembered storms when I was young as times when my family tended to huddle. We gathered radios and books, cups of tea and cookies, even if it was the middle of the night. Rules no longer applied. My father would let me stay up and watch clouds gather, or curl on the sofa in a blanket to watch television, the meteorologist waving an arm across the map of our side of the state, indicating what we were in for.

There was a knock on my door, which was so unexpected I jumped, spilling soup. I assumed, then, that it was Mrs. VanderWal coming to warn me, to invite me to their basement to take cover. When I opened it, there was my mother.

"I was driving around," she said by way of a greeting, pushing her hair out of her face, "and I could tell it was going to get nasty, so I thought I should just come here, and see if you were all right."

"I'm fine. Come on in," I said. "I was just making soup. Do you want some?"

She came in slowly, shaking off her raincoat. "This is pretty nice," she said, looking around, and I realized that, though I had given her my address over the phone, I had never invited her to visit. It seemed strange, such an oversight, yet typical of our relationship. Still, I was glad to see her.

My mother sat down at the small kitchen table while I ladled my soup. She took off her oversize glasses and cleaned the lenses on the hem of her shirt. "You know," she said, "I was worried because you told me it was the second floor. Where are you supposed to go if it gets really bad?"

"Oh, my landlord would let me come down there, I'm sure, but I don't think it's anything to worry about."

"Didn't you hear the radio?"

"Yes, but the tornado isn't even within a fifty-mile radius," I said. "I think it's just going to fizzle out and turn into a thunderstorm."

"I hope so," she said, nibbling one of the crackers I put on a plate between us.

"Remember that tornado at Grandma's?" I said.

"Of course!" my mother said. "How could I forget?"

When I was about seven years old, we were visiting my grandmother who lived two hours north. She was my father's mother, and, though we didn't visit more than three or four times a year, when they were together, there was a chumminess between them that nearly excluded my mother. I learned early on that my mother and grandmother did not adore but tolerated each other, which explained the infrequent contact. But that fall we were going to help Grandma sort through some things for her move into a condominium. I liked the word *condominium;* it sounded modern. Grandma was tired of old plumbing and cold floors, she said. But before we got started packing, a tornado warning sent us to the cellar. It was one part of the house that Grandma had neglected, claiming she was afraid of what she might find; I thought she meant bones, or rodents, but she meant only the amount of junk she had yet to deal with.

There were mountains of untouched boxes, books stacked in teetering towers, and furniture from the Depression. Against one cement wall there leaned an old bed, the box spring providing a kind of fort to hide underneath. Grandma insisted we all crawl behind it, noting that it was the safest place, being in the southwest corner of the house. But it was so cramped and smelled so awful that everyone crawled back out. My father said he thought it was safe enough just being in the cellar. We listened to a small transistor radio, static and occasional news bulletins. The tornado was nearly upon us, the newsman announced. It had demolished two farmhouses but passed right over a "branch library." I remembered thinking about that, a library made of branches, picturing an amazing structure like a tree house, with places to perch and read. I wanted the storm to end so I could go there.

My mother had brought crackers and a bottle of juice, and we finished that, happy as if it had been a feast. My grandmother produced a deck of cards from a pocket, and we sat in a circle as she dealt. Grandma loved games. We played Crazy Eights and gin rummy and one she made up called spit shine. The rules seemed arbitrary, and my mother quit out of exasperation, so the three of us played on. It seemed that we had always lived in the cellar of my grandmother's house, playing by lamplight, listening to the ominous voice on the tinny radio.

When we finally emerged, hours later, tentatively parading back upstairs, it seemed as if nothing had happened. I was vaguely disappointed. Then my father yelled from the second floor, and we raced up after him. The wall of my grandmother's bedroom had vanished. The window, a dresser, and a small rug had gone with it, but the rest of the room was strangely unharmed. Wallpaper clung to the remaining walls in tattered strips that fluttered in the calm breeze.

All my grandmother said was "Oh, my," and my mother said, "Good thing you're selling this place," which made Grandma laugh heartily. It was the first time I had seen the two of them laughing together. All of my memory of that storm became wound up in that crazy scene, the torn open room, my grandma and mother hysterical with glee. And I was astounded by the power of the weather, power that could claw open the side of a house like a giant while we blithely played cards down below.

"That room was an amazing sight," I said, remembering. We had finished our soup and were leaning over the back of my sofa and watching the sky, forgoing caution.

"I hated being down there in the cellar, cut off," my mother said. "I'm sure it was safer, but I felt like I missed something important."

"Yeah," I agreed. "It's better to see what's coming."

For the first time in a very long time, I was content just sitting with my mother, not wanting to flee, not wanting her to leave. It seemed important that we were together, huddled on my rental sofa, watching for the storm that might or might not come.

On my last day off, Lydia called to say she'd decided to throw a small cocktail party.

"It's just a few people I know, from the business," she assured me, referring to the small art community to which she belonged, "just the usual assorted group of angst-ridden chain-smokers." I supposed I would fit right in, except that I didn't paint or wield clay, or smoke, for that matter. Yet I wasn't in the mood to socialize, to "circulate."

Dill must have been breathing quietly just over my shoulder, because when I started to form an excuse to Lydia, I heard him whisper urgently, "Go." There was no time to think or to question him, so I obeyed and assured Lydia I would be there. When she told me the date, I tried not to let it register.

I arrived early, as Lydia was arranging candles everywhere as if for a séance.

"Make yourself at home," she said.

"Déjà vu," I said, attempting a joke. Lydia just kissed me on the forehead, then went off to pile her streaked blond hair atop her head and change into her party gown. I was wearing my favorite black dress, long and lean and modern, appropriate for an artists' gathering.

At ten o'clock people began drifting in, dressed festively, not one in black. Lydia introduced me to everyone as her old roommate, though it was clear this was simply a courtesy for my sake; several people came up to me, took my hand, and said, "I was so sorry to hear about your loss," or "How are you doing, *really*?" One woman noted my dress and said, "I think it's really touching that you still wear the color of mourning; most people just don't adhere to tradition anymore."

As the evening wore on, I began to seethe a little, and the mindless chatter going on around me grated on my nerves. Wishing I could go curl up on the velvet cushion, I ate a cracker and silently dared anyone to talk to me. Then Lydia brought a new arrival over for introductions.

His name was Yan, and he was a striking man, "Korean-Hawaiian," as Lydia noted in a whisper. He had only one leg, black silk pants tied at the severed knee like a package, and he leaned loosely on silver crutches that clicked against the wooden floor when he moved. He also had glittering black eyes, skin flawlessly taut, clean dashes of eyebrows.

"Yan is one of my old friends from art school," Lydia told me. "He just moved here from Chicago for a job in the art department at the college."

Yan smiled and sat down beside me, setting the crutches aside. After a moment, he said, "I heard—I'm sorry you lost your husband."

"I'm sorry you lost your leg," I blurted. Yan's eyebrows lifted slightly, and Lydia gaped at me. "I'm sorry," I muttered. "I really didn't mean that at all, it was a horrible thing to say."

"I understand," Yan said. His voice was smooth and consoling, a radio voice. "You're angry at the world. I know it isn't quite the same, but I went through that after I lost my leg. I wanted it back, couldn't believe that it was really gone. I had to go through the stages of grief, like you."

"So what stage am I in?" I demanded.

"I couldn't say," he said kindly.

A woman in a long paisley dress with a giant butterfly clip holding back her hair sat down beside us. "I think you're actually talking about the Kübler-Ross stages of dying," she said. When no one responded, she looked embarrassed for interrupting and said nothing else.

Lydia finally said, "Grief and dying have a lot in common, I think. As far as the stages go."

"So what stage am I in?" I asked again.

Lydia shrugged, held my hand. "I don't know. Are you still in denial?"

"No, I'm not," I said, then laughed in spite of myself. I thought I heard Dill laughing, too, far off, as if he were on the other side of the crowded room.

"You're stuck, Anna," Lydia said gently, turning back to me. "I say it only because I care about you so much. You'll move on soon—to anger, depression, resolution, whatever. You have to."

"Self-pity—you forgot one," Yan added, musing. The paisley friend rolled her eyes.

Lydia ignored both of them and brushed the hair from my forehead. She whispered, "Life can be good again, I really believe that. I just think you are living in Limbo."

"I like Limbo," I said.

"No, you don't, not really. You just think you do," Lydia said. I thought, She has so many philosophies about life she could start her own religion. Either that, or a radio call-in show.

Once, when I was driving home from a weekend retreat for my job, I listened to a radio program on which the host, Carmen, offered advice to the lovelorn. I liked listening to other people's private disasters; it was before I had had any of my own.

Sometimes I could tell the caller was roaming around a room, coiling and uncoiling the phone cord; I could hear the faint thud of padding feet, and sometimes the *shwoosh* of running water. It impressed me that people could be so offhand about their innermost fears and their traumas, scraping cheese sauce from plates and jamming them into a dishwasher. I also liked how some callers would punctuate nearly every sentence with her name like a chorus: *I'm not kidding, Carmen/ Look, I'm no saint, Carmen/ He really did it, Carmen/ I can't take it no more, Carmen.*

And Carmen never failed them, always offering the last word, the zinger, something you could tack onto your bulletin board to remind you day after day to get yourself together: *You walked in the door, you can walk out of it. You know what you don't want, don't you?*

When I got home, Dill was getting ready for bed, endlessly brushing his teeth and then tapping his toothbrush against the porcelain. He kissed me hello, his lips gritty with Colgate, and I told him about Carmen; it was the kind of thing I knew he would appreciate. We could lie together in the dark analyzing the callers, guess who was lying and who was telling the truth, make fun of the pseudo-Freud pretending to help them. But when I took the radio to bed with us and fiddled with the switch, Carmen was gone. In fact, there was only static, a long, thick buzzing, and after we made love, we fell asleep listening to that.

Sitting on Lydia's sofa, with the happy party noise humming around me, I could hear only static, interrupted now and then by Yan. He was no longer talking about death; now he was talking about a French film he had seen recently, concerning a knife thrower and a woman he'd rescued on a bridge.

"Excuse me," I said, and walked to the bathroom. I locked the door and stood there breathing for a few minutes in the darkened room. Then, on impulse, I stood up on the tank of the toilet and hoisted myself through the open window, landing softly on the wide, flat roof. My shoes sank a little into the thickly tarred surface as I walked across it. When I reached the edge, my toes almost in the gutter, I stood still and stared down through a network of branches, colored leaves still clinging here and there, the yards littered with brown, dry piles.

Street light bounced off the shiny bumpers of the cars parked in a line down the block. The sky was deeply dark, with a perfect little earring of a moon, the stars blinking their mysterious messages. It was another strange Indian summer, late November, and two stories below me Lydia's sprinkler swayed gently back and forth on the lawn, a limp fan of water. I took off my shoes and hurled them at it, and they landed with a satisfying, soggy thud. I looked out across the treetops, across rooftops, and imagined the people moving beyond all those other windows, watching television, eating late-night bowls of cereal, tucking restless infants back into bed, turning toward each other and making love, then sighing and falling asleep. All of those ordinary people, living their lives, sleeping their sleep, waking up to face their own corners of a new day. Innocent. Lucky.

I thought bitterly, There are no "stages" of grief; there are just rooms you keep walking in and out of, feeling your way in the darkness. Sometimes you stay in one room for a long time, sometimes you leave and come back. And you never even think to open a window to get some air. I thought again of the closed garage, the suffocating inside of the car where I'd sat with Dill, the feeling that we would never get out in time, and when we did, and I briefly believed everything would be okay, how I was crushed all over again by the news that it wouldn't. And I knew, sitting on the roof, that the thing I could never get past was the looming "What if?" What if I had fixed the garage door? What if I had gotten Dill to the hospital without the delay of running inside to dial 911?

And then, suddenly, I remembered what Jon had said. "Why didn't Dill fix the garage door?" At the time it had seemed an offhand comment, faintly critical of another man's laziness or ineptitude. But now, I saw that that wasn't what Jon had meant at all. He meant, it wasn't my fault that the garage door hadn't been fixed. People had been telling me that for months—*It wasn't your fault*—but I had always dismissed their ignorance, because I thought they were just mouthing words of comfort, trying to make me see that life is huge and incomprehensible and beyond our control and so we can't take the blame. All along I had thought they failed to see that there was one, specific thing I could have done to avert disaster, to save my husband at the last minute: If only I had fixed the door. But Jon had said simply, Why didn't *Dill* fix it? At the notion, so obvious now after all these months, I swooned.

"Why *didn't you* fix the goddamn door? Why was it always up to me to take care of everything—you had an office at home!" I raged at Dill, and I ranted at God, *Why? Why? Why?* as if the two of them were in cahoots, plotting to take away my happiness, my life. *Look at what you've done to me!*

I took deep breaths and looked over the edge of Lydia's roof and watched the sprinkler wave back and forth in the moonlight, and I wept. I couldn't have saved him. I knew it. Even if one of us had bothered to fix the spring in the garage door and I had backed the car out of the driveway and driven to the hospital, exactly the same thing would have happened, if not that day, then some other day; I would have walked out of the rest room to find Dr. Baird nervously approaching me with his terrible news. It was no one's fault. Not mine, not Dill's. There had been a small ticking bomb inside Dill's head, and no one knew it until it was too late.

Now it was one year since Dill had died, slipped away while I was in the bathroom. And a year later, as if time had twisted around and brought me right back, I had climbed out of a bathroom window and felt myself turned inside out all over again. I gripped the edge of the roof and took slow, deep breaths.

And then, he was there.

I felt him. Like so many times before, but different; this time he wasn't just a presence that could very well be imagined, he was there. All these months I had wanted so desperately for him to come back, and I believed he had. I thought that if I continued to have enough faith—like Angela Wallace—anything could happen. And the impossible happened now, but just for a bright, flickering moment. Dill slipped through me, gently as thread, as when a doctor pulls out stitches after the cut has healed. You shiver, but the pain is duller than you anticipate.

And though I couldn't see him, it was as if I were watching him drive away in a Goodwill truck with our old life in it, taillights bobbing around a bend, and then gone. As I wiped my eyes, welling once more, I was thinking:

> *There goes Dill in his flannel shirts,*
> *there goes the suit he married me in, the shoes he ran in, and*
> *   his golf stuff, though he never golfed,*
> *there goes his off-key baritone, and his deep, sharp laugh,*
> *there go his strong hands, his lean legs, his smooth chest, his*
> *   birthmark like spilled milk, his gray-green eyes,*
> *there goes the scent of Ivory soap and minty mouthwash and*
> *   Magic Markers and the smell of Dill himself and*
> *there goes his sleepy arm around me in the morning, there goes*
> *   his voice saying, "Anna, honey. Annabelle, hey, wake up."*

And when he was gone, I felt something give way, a shifting inside, like when a shelf of snow slides from a roof after the sun has shone long enough to loosen its hold.

I sat on the roof for nearly two hours. I was vaguely aware of people below leaving Lydia's house, clomping from the top-floor apartment to the street, slamming car doors, driving away. No one had seen me or come searching.

"What are you doing?" a voice shrieked. I turned around from my perch on the edge of the gutter and saw Lydia silhouetted in the small bathroom window.

"Just sitting," I said.

"Have you been out here all night?"

"I guess. I just needed to be alone for a while."

"I thought you'd left! Are you all right?" Lydia asked, her voice still overly loud and pinched with worry. "You weren't thinking about—"

I laughed. "No, I'm not going to jump, don't worry. If I did, I would probably just break my ankle and smash that shrub down there."

"Well, everyone is gone, except Yan. Do you want to come back in?" she asked, softly now. "Have some coffee with us or something?"

I stood up and walked slowly over to the window, my legs aching from stiffness. My friend looked at me, and I saw that her face was pale as the moon, her large eyes rimmed with black. A little owl. Behind her, Yan had appeared, his eyes shining at me. He reached past Lydia and poked his crutch out the window.

"Everyone needs a crutch now and then," he said gently. He smiled to indicate he knew it was a corny thing to say, but well-meant. I smiled back. When I grabbed hold of the crutch's rubber tip, Yan tugged a little, then with strong arms helped me slide back over the sill.

When I finally stood on the tiled bathroom floor, Yan hopped out of the way again and Lydia gathered me in her arms. I let her hold me for a long time. Later, she wept when she learned that it was the one-year anniversary of Dill's death, and apologized over and over for not realizing before.

"A party! Oh, God, what was I *thinking*?"

"It's okay, really," I told her. And it was.

The three of us sat in the cluttered living room on the floor and drank hot coffee. Yan began entertaining us with stories about people who had been at the party, and we laughed until we ached. Eventually, we all fell asleep curled in various positions on the floor pillows. When I woke sometime in the middle of the night, I saw that Yan's good leg was nestled against me. I didn't want to move away, but I was getting a cramp, and so I sat up. He did, too, almost immediately, as if he were tuned in to my sleep and wakefulness. He smiled at me through the dark.

"Want to talk?" he whispered.

"Sure," I said.

We sat cross-legged on the carpet, Yan with his incomplete leg forming a perfect triangle with his other. I marveled at it, at him, wondering what it was like to look down at that stump, the space below it, and wondering how he had lost it. I wasn't going to ask, but he saw me gazing at it and said, "Tree trimming."

"Really?"

"I was seventeen," he told me, "helping my father and uncle with their tree business one summer. We were all good climbers, like monkeys. This particular job was an oak tree, three hundred and fifty years old, like God himself planted it, it was so massive. I hated to see it go, you know, but it was already dead, had been for years. It was a hazard, because when the limbs become brittle and hollow, they can fall off and kill a little kid riding a bike underneath. So I was up there, cutting, and suddenly the chain saw got away from me. I had a good grip on it, but one leg slipped and somehow as I tried to recover, the blade just dove down and sliced it off. Zip! Just like that. Like it thought I was a branch." He stopped, smiling wryly, and rubbed the bump where his thigh ended. Then he went on to explain matter-of-factly how the leg had torpedoed to the ground below and landed in a nest of muddy leaves. The doctor claimed it had been "compromised" because of the dirt and length of time lapsed, and could not be reattached.

"I never forgot that he said 'compromised,' I don't know why. It seemed a funny choice of words," Yan said.

"Dill's doctor called his aneurysm a 'firecracker,' " I said.

"You have to appreciate a doctor with imagination."

We sat still for a moment. I was thinking about how animated Yan was telling his story, his personal tragedy, yet he was probably long since resigned to it. "Does it feel weird?" I asked softly.

"You mean, to touch it?" he asked, pointing to his trouser-wrapped stump. "Or the sensation of having no leg?"

"Well, both."

"No, yes, no. I don't know. Sometimes I sort of forget, I'm so used to being like *this*. Do you know what I mean?"

"Yes."

Yan smiled. "You know what's funny? Sometimes I get asked to talk to schools about art but also as a kind of inspirational speaker—they think if you're maimed you're wise. And some kid always wants to know if I kept my leg."

I started laughing, trying to be quiet and not wake Lydia. "Really? What do you *say*?"

"I tell them, 'Sure, of course. I keep it in a glass case next to my trophies.' I love the look on their faces then, picturing it—with a sock and shoe, and all the hairs."

"That's terrible!" I said.

"I know. But sometimes I wish I *did* have it. I sort of miss that little calf." He paused, musing. "I just learned to accept it, to be grateful for what was left of me."

Talking to Yan was like being with an old friend, someone I had known for a long time, not just an evening. Eventually, we grew tired again and, without a word, lay back down in the same positions as before, the darkness settling around us again like a tent zipped closed. Lydia had left windows open, and the cool air filled the room.

"It smells like camping," Yan whispered.

"It does," I said. And then we both fell quiet, thinking our own thoughts, though they seemed to overlap. As we drowsed, he took my hand and held it lightly, and I let my fingers curl into his like a shell.

A year and a day after I staggered out of the door lugging my dying husband, I went back home. I felt like someone about to enter a haunted house, tentative, the key trembling near the lock, though I wasn't really afraid. I knew there would be no ghosts here. I knew I could do this. I was just a person walking through a door, into an ordinary house.

Inside, it was musty, as to be expected, and the sunlight filtering through the haze was almost tangibly heavy. Yet, aside from the dust covering every surface, it wasn't as bad as I thought it would be. Apparently, in the first few months, Lexi and Lydia, unbeknownst to me, had come in with the spare key I'd given a neighbor for emergencies and emptied my refrigerator, washed all the dishes, and unplugged appliances. Later, as it became obvious that I had no intention of moving back home, Philip took it upon himself to contact the utility companies about rerouting bills; for nearly a year, Philip secretly had been paying my gas and electric bills, though they were low, from next to no usage. Standing in the hallway between the kitchen and living room, I thought about the safety net my friends had so silently and lovingly formed beneath and around me.

I walked to the cherry red sofa and batted the seat cushions, releasing small clouds. Then I just stood there and looked around for a long time. It was like entering a museum, the kind with roped-off rooms you walk past, eyeing with awe the remnants of a perfectly preserved era: the pen on Emily Dickinson's desk, or the cradle where Winston Churchill slept as a baby, the faintly bloodstained pillow where President Lincoln died. I sat down on the sofa and sank back, let my eyes drift over the remote control Dill had touched, a lamp he had given me for one of our anniversaries, the magazine he was reading a year ago, still folded open to the middle of an article. I picked it up without looking at the story and folded the cover back over, then continued walking through the house.

Memory shifts around in nebulous currents; you forget exactly how furniture was positioned, the color of a familiar rug. It was all the way we had left it, yet it seemed strange to me, the way a childhood home is diminished with time and one's growth. It is never the way you imagine it will be. And while I braced myself for a torrent of emotion, the waves I had been holding back for over a year, not wanting to look at the things associated with my dead husband, I was surprised to find that those things now seemed so benign, so harmless, incapable of devastating me.

When I climbed the stairs, and passed the bedroom and the study just beyond it, what finally got to me was Dill's faded purple chair sitting idly before his battered desk. I stood in the doorway, unable to cross the threshold. I felt like a person who has been through rehabilitation, taken some first weak steps, and finally begun to walk, only to find her legs giving out without warning. After taking a deep breath, though, I walked in.

I looked over the desk, pulled open drawers, sifted through files of clients without really seeing them. Then I reached for the trash can and started filling it. I hadn't planned to do it, but now it seemed the only solution. Dill was gone. His clients had long since acquired new artists and moved on. There was no one who would need these things, not even me. In no time, I had emptied three drawers, and gone to retrieve a large trash bag from the kitchen. I worked until I lost track of time, until the room grew gradually dark and I reached over to turn on the lamp. I tossed out markers and dried-up pens. I piled up designer books and color guides, unused pads of paper, and some other things I figured I could donate to someone, somewhere. By the time I finished, the room was cleared of everything but the furniture. I spun the purple chair gently and left the room, hearing the faint squeak of the swivel as I walked downstairs. I didn't look back.

For two days I labored as I hadn't in a long time. I had a newfound surge of energy, parts of me waking up as I worked. Sometimes I played music or sang, sometimes I just moved around in the silence, unbothered by it. I dusted, vacuumed, scoured and sorted. I opened all the windows, and the brisk air felt cleansing as rain. Boxes filled with Dill's clothes and shoes, science fiction books that he'd devoured and I didn't like, sports equipment, and anything else that no longer suited me. I saved a few things, of course: the desk chair, his soft blue shirt, a music box he gave me one Christmas, some photographs. I cried silently, off and on. But I didn't stop working except to sleep for a few hours on the red sofa, a blanket pulled over me. Then I rose and carried on.

Finally, I called Goodwill. My mother came over, discreetly helpful, full of gentle hints and an occasional hug. She surveyed the boxes, neatly squared in a corner of the porch, taped and labeled.

"You're so brave," she said, her smile pinched.

I thought then of the boxes in my old room, and realized, all of a sudden, that she had done the exact same thing—nearly ten years earlier—except that she hadn't gotten around to parting with them. I wondered if my father's clothes still smelled faintly of him, Old Spice and wintergreen mints, if his shoes still bore the curve of his long feet. I wondered if my mother had sat and sorted the way I had, finally determining coldly that the toiletries should be thrown out, that there was no point in keeping toothbrushes and combs, even if they still held tiny fragments of the man she loved.

I remembered a friend in college once telling me about the balloons at her niece's fourth birthday party, blown up by the girl's father that morning, and how, after he was killed in a car accident several days later, the balloons lingered for weeks, hanging by ribbons from a chandelier. My friend said that her sister, the widow, began to believe that the presence of those colored balloons, even as they shriveled and dangled limply, meant that her husband was still there somehow—his breath was inside them.

I had thought at the time the woman was crazy to believe that, a little pathetic to hold on to such a childish notion. I didn't know then what it would be like. Now I knew. And my mother knew, and as I stood with her looking over my boxes while we waited for the truck, I thought about how astonishing it is that individual people come and go on the earth every minute, but that their imprint on the few people around them is powerful and far-reaching. I reached for my mother's hand.

"We're Waiting for Godot," my mother said. I looked at her. "You know, Goodwill, Godot? It was a joke."

"Good one, Mom," I said, and laughed.

"Except I hope he actually shows up."

"He will," I said. "He said I was the last stop of the day. It's just four-thirty."

"Here he comes," she said then, and I looked down the block to see the white truck rumbling our way. She held my hand more tightly as if afraid I might not go through with it, but I squeezed hers once and let go. I walked down the steps to meet the driver.

A jolly man, old enough to be my grandfather and tall enough to have to duck in doorways, whisked in and out of the porch, whistling "My Old Kentucky Home." I asked him if he were from the South, and he laughed and said no, he was born and raised in the "You-Pee, as far north as you can get and not be Canadian, not counting Maine or Alaska, of course. Maybe Washington, too, but who's counting? Anyway, I moved down here to look for work when I was out of the service, and liked it enough to stay. So here I am."

With the last box under one arm, he smiled and turned to go. "Well," he said. "I thank you for your generous donation, ma'am. I hope it doesn't pain your heart too much to part with it." He smiled at me then in such a way that I knew, in spite of his breezy exterior, he understood what was in the boxes. I smiled back.

"Thank you," I said. "I think I'm all right."

A moment after he was gone, my mother asked, "Are you sure?"

"Yes," I said. "You want to come in?"

She shook her head. "No, I think I should get going. I have some things to do." As I watched her drive away, I had a feeling that the next time I stopped by her house, my old room would be much emptier.

When I walked back inside, my house seemed to sparkle, clean and orderly—and freezing cold. I rushed about shutting all the windows and switching on lamps. Then I twisted the knob in the gas fireplace, and watched as flames shot up. I scooted backward on the rug and sat gazing at it, hypnotized. I fell asleep there on the hearth, like an exhausted animal, and when I woke it was the middle of the night. Sitting up and stretching, I turned off the fire—such a funny thing, I thought, flames appearing and disappearing at the touch of a switch—then ambled automatically toward the stairs. It was all coming back to me, the mindless routines, routes through rooms in the dark.

I went upstairs to the bedroom and took off my clothes. I had washed the sheets and blankets, so I climbed between them like a grateful guest in my own home. First curled up on my own side, I scooted toward the middle, just a little, and reached out to touch the side that was Dill's. I knew that there would always be a hollow there, in the bed, in the house, in my life. But I could bear it. Some days better than others. It felt like driving endlessly, resting in between, and then getting up to drive some more. Sometimes you just watched the scenery flying past and barely noticed it, other days you thought you couldn't take one more minute of it. But for now I was still, and I fell asleep, my mind as clean and empty as the house.

I called Mrs. VanderWal to cancel my lease on the apartment. I had paid through the end of the month, so she had time to find another tenant. "We'll miss you," she said sweetly. "You've been one of our best renters ever. So quiet and neat. You have no idea how rare that is."

I thanked her, tempted to suggest that she post notices at the SOLO groups, where she might find another widow who would be equally invisible, but I knew she would not appreciate such morbid humor. I knew Dill would have, and there was someone else who might, too.

One afternoon two weeks after I moved back home, I answered a knock on my front door, startled to find Yan there, leaning against the porch railing. He had set his crutches aside and was balancing something large and flat against his side.

"It's a housewarming gift, or an early Christmas present," he said, smiling sheepishly. I invited him inside, intrigued. He slipped out of his coat, grasped his crutches, and looked around.

"I guess Lydia told you," I said.

"Yes. She said she had a feeling you were ready to go back home."

"Lydia often has 'feelings.'" I laughed. "But she's often right on target, I have to admit."

"So, are you doing all right?" he asked. I nodded and he smiled. "That's good." He pointed to the ice skates propped beside the door. "Going skating?"

"Just back," I said. "I go every Saturday with my friend, Celie."

"Maybe you can teach me sometime," he said. "Though I have two left feet—well, actually no left feet." He laughed.

I led him into the living room, and we sat on the sofa, the gift between us. "Open it," he said, so I did. Inside was a finished but unframed painting. I held it out at arm's length. It was filled with dark, moody colors, thick swaths of oil paint, with a bright spot over the horizon that could have been from an unseen moon or a distant sunrise. It was hard to tell. What was conspicuously clear was the sharp angle of a rooftop, surrounded by treetops, and the figure of a woman suspended in midair.

I turned to Yan. "So," I said. "Am I jumping—or flying?"

He laughed. "That's for you to decide."

"Ah, the classic response. 'Interpret it for yourself,' right?"

"Yes. But if you want to know what Lydia the optimist thinks, she said I should add wings, or a parachute. I told her that, as an artist herself, she should know better than to interfere with someone else's work, and that I want the viewer to decide for him- or herself if the glass is half empty or half full."

"And let me guess," I said. "Lydia says that, of course, it's always both. Right?"

"Right." He smiled, his black eyes sparkling at me.

"I think she's right this time," I said. Then I stood up and carried the painting to the fireplace mantel and set it on top. It covered up an antique mirror hanging there, and I thought, All the better. I liked Yan's version of me.

I thanked him for the gift as he stood to go. He pulled his crutches to his sides in one deft motion and swung himself to the door. I followed him to the porch. "See you later," I said.

He turned and smiled. "Definitely," he said. Balancing on his crutches, he tilted forward and kissed my cheek, nearly, but not quite grazing my lips. I smiled at that; it was like a small invitation to respond to later.

After he left, I closed the door and went inside to make myself a cup of tea. I pulled down the old teapot, with its gleaming brown glaze, put on the dented kettle, and watched it tremble as it began to warm. I waited until I heard the first two shrill notes of its whistle before I took it off the stove, just like I used to. Then I sat in my old spot at the table, curled my feet under the rung of the chair, and sighed. In front of me was a to-do list I had begun earlier in the day. Everything was the same and everything was different. It was as if a wave had caught hold of me and raked me underwater, where I'd been for a year, until I was tossed back onto shore in a surge of debris. And when I finally was able to catch my breath and look around with open eyes, there were moments when I actually felt grateful for what was left of me.